ONLY A

TASTE

L. MOONE

CONTENTS

CHAPTER ONE

All my belongings are neatly packed into cardboard boxes, but all I feel is chaos inside.

I don't want to go. I don't want to leave this little student flat which I've been sharing with Sarah for the past three years. But with no money or prospects, I don't have a choice.

I let out a deep sigh and sink down on the edge of the sofa.

"You alright, Mandi?" Sarah asks, handing me a cup of tea. Strong yet milky, just how I like it.

I just shrug.

"This sucks, hey." She puts her hand on my shoulder.

"Life's a bitch, especially when your family can't accept that in this country, things work a little differently," I respond.

"At least you won't have to worry about laundry. Or rent." Sarah is only half joking. Moving back home to act like the perfect Punjabi daughter to my parents will have some—admittedly small—benefits. Mostly it's a big, fat negative though.

"Yeah, I get to relive my childhood. Yay." I rest my head in my hands and try not to panic.

No more pretending to be a grown-up at twenty-three. No more staying out with Sarah—or anyone else for that matter—until the clubs close and our feet stop cooperating. No more freedom to hang out with anyone of the opposite gender, and forget about inviting a guy home with me.

Sure, I'll have a job to go to, with Mr. Gupta—Dad's friend, but that's hardly a pleasing prospect

"I'll miss you, you know." Sarah plops down next to me and puts her arm around me.

"Yeah, I'll miss you too."

"OK, this is bullshit." Sarah lets go of me and sits upright. "It's sad you have to move back in with your folks, but it's not like anyone died. They're not expecting you until tomorrow. Let's go do something!"

"Like what?" I ask, while still feeling way too sorry for myself to really care.

"I dunno. It's a nice, sunny day, I don't have anything on, neither do you. Let's just drive down to Brighton or something." *She's lost her mind.*

"And then what? I'm broke, remember? That's why I'm moving back in the first place."

"How much do you have exactly?" She grins at me expectantly.

"I dunno, about a tenner in cash, plus perhaps fifty in the bank?"

"Great! Get dressed." Sarah jumps up, visibly

excited.

I stare at her in disbelief but once she's set on something, Sarah cannot be deterred. She grabs my hand and starts dragging me off the sofa and towards the large suitcase that contains all my clothes.

"What's the plan exactly?" I wonder out loud. Does she even have a plan?

"We drive down, hang out at the beach, eat fish and chips, get a bit of a tan." She looks over at me; my skin is already pre-bronzed of course. "OK, so I'll get a bit of a tan—head to the nearest pub or whatever, get sloshed. Dance, enjoy ourselves, have a proper farewell party for you. What do you say?"

"You did hear me when I said I have literally *no money?*"

Sarah shrugs. "Since when do we have to pay for our own drinks when we go out?"

She makes a fair point. *But when we're done partying, then what?* "I'm sure even the cheapest guest house down there would wipe me out though."

"Who said anything about a guest house? I'm not planning on sleeping! Plus, we can always crash in the car."

Sometimes she has the craziest ideas. But I have to admit that the prospect of being all but grounded with my parents breathing down my neck every day is a powerful motivator to go along with her spontaneity. What have I got to lose?

"Fine. You win."

She winks at me. "Admit it, we both win."

For all my earlier grumpiness, I can't suppress a smile now. Within minutes we've thrown on colorful summer dresses—bikini underneath of course—and shoved a random collection of supplies into a pair of beach-ready canvas bags. Towel, sunscreen, sunglasses, plus a couple of books—check.

Before I have the chance to change my mind, she's herded me into her piece-of-shit car which sounds so rattly I'm surprised nothing of note has fallen off it yet. The stereo—possibly the best part of the entire car—does its best to drown out the traffic noises and creaks with loud music. I don't care what happens anymore, today I still get to be me, not who my folks expect me to be.

***

The traffic has been horrendous, and the parking situation is worse. But at last, at just after four—three hours after setting off—we finally make it to Brighton beach.

As I take my sandals off and try to follow her towards an empty spot among the sunbathing crowds, I remember why I fucking hate Brighton as a beach. Who the hell decided it's a good idea to sunbathe on rough gravel? The stones cut into my feet with every step, causing me to swear under my breath.

"What's that?" Sarah turns and asks.

"Nothing.Bloody stones." I try to tiptoe ahead, but it doesn't help. In the end I decide to put my shoes back on.

"No pain no gain, darling."

Whatever.

We manage to find a spot between some giggly teenagers and a family with a crying toddler. Not how I had wanted to spend my last afternoon of freedom, but choices are limited when the entire south of England seems to have congregated on the same stretch of stony coastline.

"Put sunscreen on me?" Sarah asks, handing me a bottle.

I do my best coating her pale back, not leaving any spots, but I already know it's hopeless. She'll be bright red within an hour, or two at the most. I would put money on it.

"Me too, please," I request when I'm done doing her.

"You sure you need it?"

"Hey, just because I have darker skin than you, doesn't mean I'm immune to cancer." I push the bottle into her hand and turn around, lifting my hair up to give her room.

"Fair point."

Soon we're both sticky, but reasonably protected

against the rays. I lie down on my towel, keeping my beach bag behind my head as sort of a pillow while I decide to make a start on the novel I brought. Sarah has other ideas though.

"Don't you want to go in the water?" she asks.

Not really, no. I shake my head and open my book to the first page.

"Come on!"

"I can't swim!" I protest.

"We won't go that far."

I put the paperback down and observe the waves, rolling in and crashing against the stones up ahead.

"Don't be a spoilsport!" Sarah insists.

"Fine. Fine! But if it's cold, I'm not doing it."

The sun is burning down onto the beach, if it wasn't for the light breeze, we'd be getting cooked. Still, the idea of cooling my toes in the water isn't so bad. Almost attractive, if it wasn't for the hellish walk to get there. Once again, I seem to have an uncanny ability to place my feet onto the sharpest rocks I can find. I'm surprised I'm not bleeding yet.

Sarah meanwhile is about ten feet ahead of me, rushing towards the sea much more eagerly, as if she's impervious to the pain of walking on hot, pokey stones.

"Oh my God, it's lovely! Not cold at all," Sarah exclaims as she takes the first steps into the water.

I soon follow, finding a definite chill travelling up

my spine when I take the first dip. Then, I must admit it's pleasantly cooling.

As soon as I'm knee-deep in the water, a wave comes and wets most of the rest of me too. I squeal, trying to regain my balance, while Sarah's laugh rings loudly in my ear. It takes all sorts of inelegant acrobatics for me not to fall over. I can just imagine the spectacle that must have been; me trying to balance my rather solidly built frame in the waves.

"Very funny," I remark dryly, while Sarah continues to giggle at me.

"It was. You should've seen yourself."

Emboldened by a desire for revenge, I take a few steps in her direction and try to splash water at her. She promptly dives down under the water, evading me and wetting the rest of her body in the process, ruining my plans. *No matter, I'll get you sooner or later!*

When she pops up again, she gives me a wide smile.

"See? It's fun!"

Another wave rolls in and she paddles along with it effortlessly, while I'm again almost thrown off my feet. But I refuse to go in further where the waves are less intense. Just because I'm grumpy about moving back home doesn't mean I'm ready to drown myself.

Five, maybe ten minutes pass while we continue to soak ourselves. It occurs to me that our stuff is sitting unguarded in a crowd of strangers, and I decide to head back.

"You enjoy yourself. I'm going to read now," I call out to Sarah, who has gotten distracted by a stray volleyball, thrown in her direction by a group of guys also enjoying the waves.

"Fine, see ya!" She waves at me, then throws the ball back to one of them. Well, I guess she's not going to get bored at this rate.

I'm in the process of limping back to my towel, when my stomach starts to growl. Of course, in our hurry to get out of the house, neither of us bothered with lunch, nor packed any snacks. A quick scan of the surrounding area reveals that the only thing somewhat nearby is a food truck close to where we left the boulevard. That's one hell of a walk.

Needs must, so I grudgingly take my wallet and phone out of my bag and go on limping over the hot stones. Why couldn't we have gone to a sandy beach instead?

CHAPTER TWO: CALLUM

"Mr. Byrne, I can assure you that you won't find a better location for your new restaurant in all of Brighton." The estate agent flashes his extra-white teeth. He looks almost like a shark, readying himself to tear his prey to pieces—me in this case.

"The rent is too high; it won't be viable," I argue, while looking around the empty building again. A lot of decorating would be needed as well. It's too much.

"Think of the footfall!" He points out the window which is currently partially obscured by white paint. Still, masses of day-trippers can be seen from where we stand.

"How about you speak to the owners again and let me know if the lease is negotiable? It will take a lot of investment to bring this property up to scratch." I offer him my hand, signaling the end of the viewing, as well as the discussion. If he comes down enough, I may consider this property, otherwise, it's back to the drawing board.

"Very well. Thank you very much for your time." The estate agent shakes my hand slightly less enthusiastically than at the beginning of the meeting.

After leaving the empty shop, we say our goodbyes

and go our separate ways.

It's a beautiful day, deep blue skies with not a cloud in sight. Warm too, the surging temperatures of our current summer heat wave evident in the amount of exposed skin outside. Apparently, I'm overdressed. Swimming trunks and bikinis, that's Brighton's dress code in the summer. I stand out like a sore thumb in my jeans and button-up shirt.

The footfall would be good here, though I'd expect my new restaurant to quickly become bookings-only once the new show airs. Perhaps I should consider a location that's a little further away from the madding crowds, and hopefully more affordable. I don't want to have to shutter up the place as soon as I'm no longer on TV.

Enough work for one day though. Today is too lovely to waste.

The beach is crowded. So much so, I'm not at all tempted to go near it. Perhaps if I walk further out towards the western side of town I'll find some peace and quiet. But not without sampling some of the local refreshments. The only establishment not selling fish and chips around here seems to be the ice cream truck parked up on the pavement. There's a queue of people already waiting, but I can't help myself. Gelato will do that to a person.

I join one of the two queues and wait my turn. It takes a while, but it'll be worth it.

ONLY A TASTE

"One scoop of rum and raisin, please," I say, shocked to find that the young woman to my left has word-for-word ordered the exact same thing. The two guys behind the counter look at each other and pause.

"Okay, you're going to have to sort this out between yourselves," my guy says. "We've only got one scoop left."

Looking over at my competition, I'm struck by her striking feminine beauty. Big brown eyes gaze up at me, a mixture of disappointment and hope. Her full lips half-parted as if she's about to say something, but something interrupted her. I find myself uncharacteristically reluctant to speak up first, but it looks like I have no choice.

"Let's flip a coin for it," I attempt a joke.

Her stare tells me I failed. My eyes are quickly drawn to her hand, clutching a purple leather wallet. No ring, no tan line where one might have been. She looks pretty young, but not inappropriately so.

"I can just get something else," she whispers at last. Her eyes are still glued to me. Did she recognize me and that's why she's staring? Or is it something else? Have I got something stuck in my teeth?

"I hope you won't take this the wrong way." I pause, while she raises an eyebrow.

My guy, who decided to serve the customer behind me instead of waiting for us to resolve our gelato stand-off, pauses mid-conversation. He's clearly listening in to our exchange.

The black-haired beauty patiently waits for me to finish, but something in her body language has changed. I'm sure she gets this all the time. Fuck, I feel like a creep for even trying.

"You have it." I turn to face the chalkboard again, ready to pick another flavor. "I'll have tiramisu," I tell the guy behind the counter, who just shrugs. I guess he was looking forward to watching me get shot down, had I actually made a move.

Meanwhile, the younger guy hands the woman her scoop of rum and raisin in a cone, which she accepts with a smile. God, what a radiant smile. She takes her change and turns, walking off towards the beach. I quickly take my cup and impossibly tiny spoon and rush after her.

"Excuse me, miss," I say, when I catch up with her a few steps ahead.

She turns and stares at me again. How the hell do I do this without coming across like a total douche bag? Funnily enough, coming across like a douche has never been much of a concern. You win some you lose some, and ever since the first season of my show aired years ago, I haven't really had to work hard to get female attention. But there's something different about this one. I wonder if much of my interest in her is caused by how hard she's making things?

"Yes?" she asks, sounding stand-offish. Her rich

amber-colored eyes are too distracting, I almost forget what I was about to say.

"I was wondering if I could take you out to dinner?" I ask at last.

She scrutinizes me from head to toe, as she considers the question. Perhaps she's wondering if it's worth the sacrifice to stick the ice cream in my face.

"Do I know you from somewhere?" she says finally.

Normally, I may have been more than happy to explain, but not this time. *Oh yeah, I'm on TV*, seems way too tacky. So I shrug. "Maybe I just have one of those faces?"

My answer makes her pause as she cocks her head and looks me right in the eye. Shit, she can tell I'm bullshitting her.

"Where would you take me?" She has a lick of ice cream, rescuing some droplets that were about to dribble off the side of the cone.

I hadn't thought that far ahead. What is it about this woman that she throws me off so much?

"That entirely depends on what type of food you like."

A hint of a smile plays on her lips.

"I'm here with a friend. Is she invited for dinner as well?"

Crap .

Finally a full grin does appear on her face. "No

need to look so shocked, I'm only joking."

I smile back at her, relieved to have not made a complete ass of myself. Yet.

"But I'd better let her know anyway." She turns to scan the beach stretching out ahead of us, before facing me again. "So. What time and where?"

"Nine? Here? Unless you have a better idea."

"Bear in mind I'm only here for the day, so I don't have a change of clothes with me. What you see is what you get, I'm afraid." She glances down at herself, smoothing down the multi-colored cotton summer dress that covers what appears to be a bikini. And curves; ample curves as far as the eye can see. I shouldn't stare. No matter how tempting. God, she's beautiful.

"No matter, same here." I suddenly realize I don't even know her name. "I'm Callum, by the way." In the absence of a better idea of what to do, I stretch out my hand towards her.

She accepts the handshake, though the slight curl of the corners of her mouth suggests I did indeed just make an ass of myself at last.

"Mandi. *Lovely* to meet you." Yep, her tone confirms it. *Ouch.*

I try to think of something else to say to break the tension, or at least to distract me from the instant reaction I feel upon touching her hand. What is it about her? You'd think I'd never interacted with a beautiful woman before. How is it that she makes me feel more like an awkward teenager than a grown-ass and dare I say successful man in his thirties?

"Perhaps we should exchange phone numbers, so we don't miss each other in the crowds here," I mumble, while quickly pulling my hand back and fishing my mobile out of my pocket.

"Sure," she says, before giving me her number. When we say our goodbyes immediately after, I can't help wondering if I'll ever see her again, or she'll decide she'd much rather vanish with her supposed friend. Only time will tell.

CHAPTER THREE

"Oh, you're done swimming," I remark, as I lower myself onto my towel.

Sarah looks up from her phone, her expression brightening immediately when she notices the half-eaten cone in my hand. "Ice cream! Where?"

I point back towards where I had just come from, the truck. "Up there. Anyway, so listen. The funniest thing just happened." I proceed to tell a severely distracted Sarah all about the guy, Callum.

"Seriously hot though. Like *seriously*," I finish. His dreamy blue eyes and weather-ruffled blond hair are hard to forget, as was the obviously toned body which his fitted white shirt didn't obscure as much as emphasize. Although he looked a few years older than me, there was something boyish and innocent about him.

Sarah looks like I've got her attention again and she's over her gelato craving, at least for the moment.

"And you think you know him from somewhere?" she asks.

I nod slowly, still unable to place him. "Yeah, it's driving me crazy. And he was no help whatsoever."

"Oh well, maybe you'll figure it out on your date."

"I guess that means I have to actually turn up, eh?"

"What, you planned not to?" Sarah's eyes are close to popping out as she stares at me.

"Well, it doesn't seem fair for you to be on your own." I shrug, trying to rid myself of the feeling that I really would like to see this guy again.

"Bitch, please! This is your farewell party of sorts. You think your folks will let you go on dates with hot strangers when you move back?"

Her remark hurts, because it's true. No. I don't expect they'd let me go on dates, and especially not if the guy in question is *white*.

"So that settles it then." Sarah rests her hand on my shoulder. "You go have fun, I'm sure I can entertain myself. In fact, did you see the guys who were swimming at the same time as us?" A mysterious smile forms on her lips.

"Yeah?"

"One of them seemed quite, you know... interested. They asked if I wanted to join them at some local club tonight. I was planning on asking you, but I'm sure it'll be fun even if I tag along on my own." Sarah lets go of me and lies back on her towel, putting her sunglasses over her face, still smiling to herself.

"If you're absolutely sure..." I say.

She waves away my remark. "I can take care of myself. And if not, I totally intend to let the guy in the red and black swimming trunks have a go at taking care of me. Plus, you can always join us if the date bombs."

I let out a giggle and she joins in too.

"Slut."

"Whore."

She raises her hand and I give her a high five before lying back on my own towel as well. Tonight is going to be awesome. I can't wait until nine o'clock. Let's hope this book is interesting enough to make the time pass quickly.

***

"So, I'll see you when I see you," I say, while waving at Sarah, who is staying behind at the beach until the group she's joining for the evening is going to leave.

"Have a great one. Make it count!" She winks at me, making me smile. Yes, I intend to make it count indeed. This could be the last time in a long while I'll get to enjoy myself. Let's hope the guy, Callum, doesn't turn out to be a freak.

When I walk up the steps towards the boulevard, it's three minutes past nine. Hopefully that's late enough not to seem desperate, and punctual enough for him to actually be there waiting for me. Assuming he's punctual.

It's busy, as it has been all day, and it takes me a

moment to find him in the crowd. His face lights up in a smile when he spots me.

"Hey!" I say, smiling back at him. Oh God, this is going to be awkward, isn't it?

"You made it," he responds, hesitating for a moment, before leaning in and giving me a peck on the cheek.

Good job, much better than the weird handshake earlier.

"Said I would, didn't I?" Ignoring the fact that he's got Sarah's insistence to thank for my presence.

"Your friend, she's okay being on her own tonight?" The slight lilt in his accent is endearing, I wonder where he's from originally? He doesn't sound English.

"Oh, Sarah. She has a knack for finding company wherever she goes." I look around at the busy street leading off from the coastline, wondering if that's where we're headed. "So where are you taking me?"

"I've got a few options. What sort of food do you like?" Callum asks. How very attentive of him to ask.

"Anything is fine, I'm not picky. Surprise me."

I don't know why I don't just say the first food that pops into my head: Italian. Part of me wants to see what he'll come up with when it's purely down to him. He seems to want to impress me, so I let him.

He nods, then offers me his arm which I accept. A nice, gentlemanly gesture. I glance over at him. That face. I know his face from somewhere and I still can't remember from where. It's infuriating.

"I love Brighton," he remarks, as we start on our walk up the narrow streets. "It's just so colorful."

"Yeah, it's not bad. Too many people, though."

A lot of the shops have already shut, leaving only the eateries and bars open. Still, the sun is burning down brightly, sunset is still some time away, which always makes summers seem surreal to me. It looks like it's daytime, when in fact it's almost time for the nightlife to start.

My stomach growls painfully, reminding me of the fact that I've had nothing but a gelato for lunch today, as Callum pauses outside a rather cozy looking bistro. That was quick!

"Outside or in?" he asks, eyeing the tables that line the pavement beside us.

"Outside, obviously."

He pulls out a chair for me, before seating himself. Almost immediately, a waitress arrives with two menus.

"Here you go, sir." She hands him the leather-bound folder, and then stares. And stares. And continues to stare even as she gives me the other one.

"Thank you." Callum starts leafing through the pages, and it's only then that the waitress catches herself, blushes a deep red and rushes off back inside.

"That was weird." I turn around to watch her

almost run into the 'Staff Only' door at the back of the small restaurant.

"What?"

"Oh, the waitress. She looked like she'd seen a ghost."

Callum chuckles, then goes back to inspecting the offerings.

Wonder what all that was about? And he didn't seem all that surprised either, which is bizarre. Where the hell do I know his face from?

The menu is simple, mostly French-inspired with hints of Mediterranean cuisine here and there. There aren't a lot of options, four main courses, six starters, and yet it all looks tempting and I can't decide.

"What are you having?"

"I've read that the lamb is great here." Callum hovers his finger over the page, then looks up at me. "You?"

"I guess the fish, since we're at the seaside?"

"Good choice. Wine?"

"Oh, you pick. I don't know much about wine." I close the menu and look over at Callum. He *is* gorgeous. Let's hope we get past the initial weirdness soon.

"Now that that's out of the way..." Callum sits back and we make eye contact for the first time since reaching our destination. I can't deny that there's something there, a promising spark. "Tell me about yourself? What do you do?"

"Oh..." I think for a moment, wondering whether to be honest or not. "I *was* a student, but I've got my degree now and have been looking for work. Unsuccessfully, I might add."

"Okay, what did you study?" His eyes are fixed on mine, and I dare not look away.

"Business administration, specializing in finance."

"That sounds pretty serious." He smiles briefly.

I wonder if I've intimidated him. A lot of guys hate it when they think you're smarter than they are.

"I guess so. Not that it helped me find work. This is actually sort of a historic night for me." I avert my gaze, kicking myself that I'm even bringing this up. I'm supposed to be enjoying myself, not venting to a complete stranger! Rule No. 1 of one night stands: don't bring your baggage into it.

"How's that?"

Shall I steer the conversation in another direction? Make something up? I look up again, noting the concern in his eyes. He seems to really want to know...

"I'm actually moving back in with my folks tomorrow. One of Dad's friends is offering me a bookkeeping job in his company. Not quite what I had hoped for, but better than nothing."

He frowns. "I see. Perhaps it's just temporary, until you find something else."

ONLY A TASTE

I smile at his attempt to comfort me, but I already know the only way I'll get to move on is if I get married first, and that's something I'm really not ready for.

"Anyway, enough of that. I'm sure you didn't ask me out here to listen to me whine about my life." I nod thanks at the waitress, who has just arrived with two glasses and a bottle of whatever wine Callum picked out. She's fucking staring at him again and it's starting to get on my nerves.

"Are you ready to order?" she finally says, while fumbling with her notepad and pen.

I'm too pissed off to say anything, so Callum steps in to order for the both of us. She blushes again, thanks him and vanishes.

Seriously? Am I fucking invisible? What is her problem? I get that he's hot, but hey, he's here with *me*, isn't he?

"So, how about you? What do you do?" I ask, hoping to rid myself of any lingering annoyance now that we're alone again.

CHAPTER FOUR: CALLUM

"What do you do?" Mandi's voice sounds a little choked, perhaps she's feeling much more down about moving in with her parents than she let on initially. She seems bright, well educated. Surely she'll get her break, even if it doesn't seem like it right now.

Anyway, what did she ask? Oh shit, what do I do?

"I'm a chef," I finally say.

She stares at me for a moment, her eyebrows pulled together into a half-frown.

"A chef..." Then her eyes widen. Oh dear, there it is. The moment of recognition.

"Oh fuck!" she exclaims, covering her mouth with her hand as soon as she catches herself.

"Sorry, I'm just... Okay, now I get why that waitress kept staring at you. Callum... Of course. God, I feel pretty silly now."

I grin at her, hoping that the awkwardness will wear off soon enough. "Sorry about that, I should have been upfront when you asked earlier—"

"Where I'd seen you before. It's been driving me crazy, I couldn't figure it out! I kept thinking have we met somewhere and I just didn't remember it properly? TV didn't even come into it." She picks up her glass and takes a generous sip of wine to deflect.

"I didn't want to be all 'so, I'm on TV' and come across like a total dick."

Thankfully, my remark has the desired effect. She bursts out laughing and sets the glass down again.

"Yeah, that would have been weird. Point taken."

Encouraged by her reaction, I decide to take the humor to the next level. "Anyway, it was refreshing, having to work for this dinner date. Thanks for that."

In a fraction of a second, her smile vanishes and she just stares at me. Shit, that went too far, didn't it? "What do you mean, ' *work for it*'?"

"Uhm... You know... You didn't make it easy, that's all," I explain, certain I've just dug a deeper hole for myself.

Then she grins again, brushing her hand past mine in the centre of the table.

"Oh God, you're so easy to wind up!" She takes another sip of wine and leans back into her chair, her eyes completely relaxed now.

"Well, you're impossible." I smile back at her. This one is something else. Hilarious, if only I wasn't so damn off my game with her.

"Your food." The flustered waitress is back, setting down our cold starters ahead of us. "Umm... If you don't mind me asking..."

I look up only to find her staring at me with a look of adoration on her face. That's what Mandi meant.

She's clearly a fan and I'm too used to it to realize how weird this must be for everyone involved.

"Yes?" I ask.

The waitress looks down at her hands, then quickly retrieves the notepad from the pocket of her apron. "Could I have your autograph? It would mean a lot. I watch your show all the time..."

I smile at her, then glance at Mandi, who is just observing the scene with an incredulous look on her face.

"Sure." I take the pad and pen and start. "What's your name?"

"Maria."

To Maria, lovely to meet you. Callum Byrne

"Here." I hand her the completed note.

"Thanks so much!" She grabs the pad and rushes back inside.

"I get it now, but that's still so bizarre," Mandi remarks.

"Sorry about that." I smile, then lean forward, admiring the presentation of the food in front of me. Not bad. This place truly is a hidden gem.

"Full marks for being all nice about it, I would find it hard. Especially if it happens a lot."

"It was a learning curve at first, but I'm getting better at dealing with being recognized. Still very refreshing not to be though. Kudos to you." I wink at Mandi, then pick up a fork, ready to attack the food.

"Bon appétit."

"Likewise." From the corner of my eye, I see her hesitating to start on her own food. "You know, I'm sorry for commenting."

"Not at all." *Lovely.* The fresh flavor of coriander makes this salad stand out. The reviews were right about this place.

"No, I feel I must be totally honest. I was a bit annoyed earlier, before, you know. She was just staring at you, like... It makes sense now." I look up, finding Mandi looking just a little bit flustered herself.

"Sounds like you were jealous," I blurt out before catching myself.

"I wouldn't say jealous *per se*." Mandi looks away for a moment, brushing a lock of her thick blackish brown hair behind her ear.

"Yeah, you were!" I say, emboldened when I notice the slight curl in the corner of her lip. She's all about the subtle cues which most guys would never notice.

"Okay! Jeez. I give up." She throws her hands in the air in defeat, then looks straight at me again and I know my gamble has paid off.

It makes sense now, I know what to do. Games won't work on her, neither will self-censorship and false niceties. No, with her somehow I have to let the real me out for a change. Uncensored. Anything less won't do the job.

Rather than feel out of my depth like before, I'm relieved. It's time to take off the mask and let her see the Callum Byrne they'd never air on TV.

"This food is lovely," Mandi remarks, as she takes another bite. "I probably shouldn't be so surprised."

"They don't just keep me around for my charming personality and good looks, you know. I do know my food."

"I wouldn't know, I don't really like cooking shows." *Ouch*, her honesty is refreshing to the point of bluntness and I like it. What a change from the women I usually end up meeting, who are already fawning before I even say a word. It takes a lot more than cheap fame to impress Mandi, yet I'm not discouraged. Far from it.

She glances at me through her full black lashes, her gaze lingering on me just a little bit longer than before. My eyes are drawn to the curvature of her full lips, before I catch myself.

"Fair enough." I take a sip of wine, then return to her lingering eyes again. "What *do* you like? What do you do for fun?"

"This is going to sound really stupid." She plucks off a piece of bread, before dipping it into the juices left on her plate and putting it in her mouth, chewing thoughtfully. Again, those inviting lips, how they beg to be kissed. It takes a lot for me stop staring and continue the conversation.

"Try me."

"Crochet."

My glass is halfway between the table and me, when I put it back down again without taking a second sip. "Wait, what?"

"Told you it's stupid. But I really enjoy it. It's creative as well as useful and it relaxes me." *Is she joking?* She looks completely serious this time.

"Not stupid at all when you put it like that, but just not something I imagined someone like you would enjoy. My grandma used to crochet."

She shrugs, then smiles widely at me. "I'm only kidding."

"Really? You totally had me."

"I don't think crochet is stupid. Funnily it was *my* grandma who taught me, actually. We're very close." She grins at me, clearly unapologetic about her unusual hobby. Though she is undeniably beautiful, it's her confidence that makes the biggest impression on me. She seems completely comfortable with who she is. And that smile... I can't get enough of her smile.

Yep, she's completely unlike the women I usually end up dating. In every possible way. She's real in a way that most people around me are not.

"Oh well, I have no right to talk. Growing up, I was the boy who would rather lock himself in the kitchen than go out and play football with other kids."

"So uncool," she teases.

"Oh yeah. Very. Luckily for me, it turned out okay."

"A toast. To us, being really uncool."Mandi raises her glass, and I follow her lead. Refreshing, indeed.

"I'll drink to that. How was the wine anyway? Ready for another bottle?"

She nods. I feel like I'm getting better at reading her, or perhaps that's just the wine deceiving me. Either way, she looks like she's enjoying herself, which is a relief.

I'm not used to worrying about what people think of me. Tonight though, I not only want to be my uncensored self, I want her to like me for it.

"So you and your grandma were close, then?" I ask, for lack of a better question.

"Still are. Mom and Dad are always busy working."

"If you don't mind me asking," I start, hoping she won't take my question the wrong way. Her inquisitive eyes encourage me to continue. "Where are you from?"

"Langley, near Slough. Born and raised."

I nod, I'd spent a short while living in Slough after coming over from Ireland, so I know the area. "And your family?"

"Punjab, India." She looks away for a brief moment, making me wonder whether she did find my question uncomfortable.

"Beautiful country," I remark, remembering mainly the food I'd sampled on my various trips to India.

She just shrugs, then looks me in the eye again. "I wouldn't know."

"Don't tell me you've never been?" I exclaim, almost offended on her behalf.

"Well—" Mandi starts, but we are interrupted by the presence of the same waitress from before, along with a man dressed in a chef's uniform, one looking even more flustered than the other.

"I'm sorry to interrupt," the chef starts, while wiping his hands nervously on his apron.

"Not at all," I say.

"I was just wondering if the food was to your liking, Mr. Byrne?"

"Very nice. I enjoyed it very much, how about you, Mandi?" I ask, noting she's again very subtly showing signs of disbelief or frustration, I can't quite tell yet which, perhaps both.

"Amazing," she says, while folding her hands and looking up at the two intruders.

"Thank you, thank you, I'm glad to hear it. I was just wondering something else... Ehh..." He scratches his forehead, then fidgets with both of his hands. "This is just a small family business, you see, and I was wondering if Maria here would be permitted to take your picture? We have a whole wall inside with photographs of previous guests, and we would love to capture this moment right here, with you... and your lovely companion."

I smile patiently and nod. It's not the first time, neither will it be the last. Whenever I visit any eatery not directly affiliated to me, it's very common to be asked for a photograph by the staff.

"Wonderful, please smile!" the chef says, while the waitress takes out her smart phone and awkwardly takes a shot of Mandi and me. As I look over, she's not only, not smiling as requested, she looks like someone's about to pull a tooth or worse. Shit, this is uncomfortable, dragging her into the weirdness of my everyday life.

CHAPTER FIVE

Well, this is bizarre. The whole thing, with just the waitress at first, then even the chef who especially came out of the kitchen to talk to Callum... I don't know how he deals with it on a regular basis, because I'd be hopeless.

I look over at him as he first gives the chef, then Maria the waitress a friendly handshake. He smiles at me apologetically when they finally leave again. I admire how patient he is about all this.

"Sorry about that."

"The price of fame, eh?" I remark, while playing around with the last bit of purple frilly lettuce on my otherwise empty plate.

"Yep."

"This sort of thing happens all the time?" I ask, wondering why otherwise sane and rational grown-ups would act like blushing teenagers around someone, simply because they've been on TV. While he's gorgeous and probably cooks well enough, he seems to be just a regular guy. Why go all gaga in his presence, then?

And then I remember how Sarah gets when some big-time writer or blogger comments on one of her articles, and I wonder if perhaps I'm the odd one out for being too utterly dry to become anyone's fan. The obligatory boy band obsession from my teenage years I'll conveniently ignore. It doesn't count. Teenagers *aren't* sane.

"All the time," he confirms, looking away at nothing in particular.

Our meal is interrupted by a few more moments of awkwardness with Maria the waitress when she brings us our wine refill and main courses. In the meantime Callum tells me all about the new restaurant he's planning to open here in Brighton.

As he enthusiastically lays out his plans, it becomes clear that his new venue will be a very different affair from the little takeaway Mom and Dad run, with the help of my brother, Jai.

Callum's passion shows though in his words. It's obvious he really does love what he does in a way that I'll probably never know for myself. I've never met anyone who was even half as passionate about finance. Even for my classmates at university, it always seemed like the subjects we studied were a means to a greater end: finding a highly paid job.

I hesitate to mention Mom and Dad's takeaway at all, considering I've never really been into the whole catering thing and don't want to give the impression that I'm only bringing it up in order to keep up appearances. The truth is, I might as well be a complete layman when it comes to the restaurant business, and that's fine by me.

After some pressing from his side, I do at last let my guard down and tell Callum all about what I really wanted to do with my life: become an interior designer. If it wasn't for my parents disagreeing with those plans, and strongly steering me towards something more serious, that is.

Although I hadn't planned to share so much about myself, the way he seems to hang on every word of mine makes me reconsider. It's strange, how after chatting for just an hour, you can feel closer to someone who is actually still a total stranger. The way our conversation flows, it's almost as if we've become friends already. Friends who are hopefully heading for some *benefits*.

"Say, what were your plans for after the meal?" I ask, wishing desperately for him to get over with the small talk and get his flirt on properly. I'm eager to celebrate my last night of freedom in every way possible.

"I'm going to assume that there's nowhere you have to be for a while?" he asks.

"Free as a bird. Just for tonight."

He considers my words, hopefully catching their hidden meaning.

"We best make the most of that then." He gives me a stare that suggests he did get my drift. Nice.

Perhaps now we can get over the *date* part of the evening and onto that tasty stuff you only get to when a date goes well, or when you didn't really have long-term intentions at all.

Shit, I hope he doesn't think this is a proper first date?!

"I just want to make something clear," I start.

He nods once while rubbing his chin, yet never breaks eye contact. It's putting me on edge but I try not to let it show.

"I've touched upon how things are a bit complicated for me right now. So I'm not *looking* for anything, all right? I just want to have fun tonight."

He presses his lips together tighter, as if trying to prevent himself from making a smart-ass remark.

"I can live with that, on one condition."

"Yes?" I ask.

"Let's see where the night goes and keep an open mind."

I open my mouth in protest, I know exactly where this can go: beyond hopefully a shared bed for a few hours, it can't go anywhere else.

"Shh... That's my condition, and I'm sticking to it."

I sigh in defeat, realizing he's probably not going to back down. "Fine. I'll keep an open mind." Not that it'll do me much good. From tomorrow, no matter what my supposedly open mind has decided about Callum, my folks will make the decision for me.

"I feel like I owe you a gelato, or some other

dessert," I tease, while pushing my creaky chair back.

He scrutinizes me, looking for the subtext in my words. "I'm sure we can work something out." Callum leaves a generous tip on the table, before offering me his arm.

We walk for a while, through the streets which have gone from crowded to quieter to crowded again now that the day trippers have turned into partygoers. We pass by pub after pub, resisting live music trying to invite us inside. It's an easy choice—at least for me—I'd rather have alone time with him than be surrounded by drunken revelers.

By the time night sets in, we're back at the boulevard, Callum's arm protectively around my shoulders as we enjoy the view. Now that it's dark, the sea is mostly invisible. The one thing left to light it up are the twinkling lights of Brighton pier, jutting out from the coast and into the calm waters. Of course his hand resting on top of my arm is distracting me. His body next to mine is begging to be the sole focus of my attention.

It's there, with a backdrop of city lights to my right and the dark waters of the English Channel to my left, that he makes his move. He takes both my hands as we stand face to face, his features barely lit up by the streetlights, though I can see him well enough to understand the intention in his eyes.

I raise myself slightly, and he wraps one arm

around my waist, supporting me, drawing me closer. His cologne smells fresh and inviting. His eyes linger on my lips for a painfully long moment, until he moves in for the kill.

Usually, I'm never this involved, this overwhelmed by the presence of a guy I've only just met. My eyes shut when his lips touch mine, and my heart seems to somersault in my chest. For just a moment, I forget what lies ahead tomorrow, and just feel privileged to have this moment with him.

"Shall we call it a night?" I ask, once I've regained my composure. It's odd, the imbalance I feel. I could float away if it wasn't for Callum holding on to me.

"Already?" He never once breaks eye contact. Why the question, though? I figured the kiss meant he's interested.

"Assuming you want to take things further, I figured it would be best not to have an audience," I remark, while nodding over to the side at the group of teenagers hanging around a couple of scooters shooting looks in our direction.

"What about dessert?" His previously brilliant blue eyes have turned a deep, dark black in this light.

"Exactly." I couldn't look away if I wanted to; he captivates me.

"I have an idea, follow me." Callum breaks the spell and takes my hand, leading me through the narrow streets once more. With anyone else I might question where we're headed, or what the plan is. Somehow, with Callum, I don't feel the need to be in control. We pass through the busiest part of town into a quieter alleyway and pause in front of an unassuming restaurant.

"Wait here." Before I get the chance to respond, he disappears inside, leaving me wondering what he's up to. Through the window I can see that the place is mostly empty, possibly they're planning to close up soon.

He's talking to a middle-aged man whose black hair and olive skin hint at a Mediterranean heritage. After some back and forth, the man nods and heads into what I presume must be the kitchen. Callum, meanwhile, gets his phone out and makes a call.

What is he doing? If only I could read lips.

By the time he's finished with the phone, the man—who I'm guessing is in charge of the restaurant—comes back carrying a cardboard bag.

Callum fishes his wallet out of the back pocket of his jeans, and a friendly argument ensues, ending when Callum finally tucks a few notes into the restaurant owner's shirt pocket. They shake hands and out he comes.

"Sorry, hope you didn't get bored waiting."

I shoot him a suspicious smile and eye the fancy bag with the gold printed logo in his hand. It looks a lot less like a takeaway bag than something one might get at an expensive boutique.

"Do I get to ask?"

Callum smiles and shakes his head. "It's a surprise."

"Now where to?" I ask.

He gestures back to where we had just come from. "Not much further now."

Again, he takes my hand, and we walk for another five minutes until the sea comes back into view further up ahead and we pause in front of a charming Victorian villa that's been converted into a hotel.

"After you," Callum says, holding the door open for me. I'm impressed that the reception is still open, even more impressed that a place like this would even have a vacancy on what has got to be one of the busiest times of the year in Brighton.

I step inside and am greeted by a proper-looking gentleman who looks to be in his seventies. Like a throwback to another era, he's wearing an old fashioned three-piece suit, including a golden pocket watch. The interior of the hotel seems to match, with period-correct wallpaper and a huge crystal chandelier lighting up the lobby.

"Welcome! Your room has been prepared. If there's anything else I can assist you with, don't hesitate to ring the bell."

"Thank you, Cecil. Good night." Callum takes the key from the old man's outstretched hand and leads me up the ornate wooden staircase that winds around the back of the reception desk. Another few flights of stairs later—thankfully I'm wearing sensible sandals today—and we stop in front of what I assume to be our room.

He slips the key into a teak wood door, and steps back, leaving it slightly ajar.

"Go on," he says.

I push the door wide open and am speechless. The room isn't very big, but the decor more than makes up for that. And the view, oh my, the view. The four-poster bed in the centre of the room is perfectly positioned in front of a balcony which overlooks the coastline.

"Wow." It's all I can say. I've never thought of myself as the romantic type, but I can't deny I'm impressed.

"Beautiful, isn't it?" Callum says, pulling the door shut behind him. That accent; is my mind playing tricks on me or has his accent become more pronounced compared to earlier tonight?

"Breathtaking."

I awkwardly wait by the bed for him to join me, trying desperately to regain my composure. It's no use though, my heart is hammering in my throat and I don't know where to look anymore.

"As are you," he says, placing his hand on the side of my neck, drawing me closer for a kiss which reduces the remainder of my defenses to rubble.

CHAPTER SIX : CALLUM

"Breathtaking," Mandi says. She can hardly take her eyes off the view.

"As are you." Her reaction is clear, the most guarded person I've ever met is impressed, in her own way.

The look of wonder and amazement in her eyes is almost better than all the smiles I managed to inspire this evening.

I can't take it anymore and move in for another kiss. The first one at the beach side had left me wanting throughout our walk to get here.

She sighs into my lips, and her body seems to give in to me completely.

I want her, my God, I want her so badly it makes my skin ache. I leave the bag containing our desserts on the bedside table and reach out for her.

Our lips fuse hungrily, both of us equally eager for things to progress. She and I are on the same page now, desperate for the night to claim us.

Finally, after holding back before, I sense the time has come to leave words behind and express ourselves by touch. I run my hands over her back, exploring her elegant shoulders, the curvature of her spine, down towards her generous buttocks. She doesn't stop me, rather she melts against me, pressing her body into mine, as her hands start on their own little journey of discovery.

Every touch of hers sets me alight, almost singeing my skin as well as soothing it. Looking into her endless eyes, I see a reflection of my own lust.

"I want you," I hear myself say with a voice so raw it's almost unrecognizable as my own.

She doesn't respond, at least not using words, instead she hooks her fingers into the belt loops of my jeans and tugs at it. She yearns for more closeness, as do I.

I run my fingertips over her naked shoulders, teasing the straps of her dress downward, then kissing the freshly exposed skin left behind. She shivers, then starts unbuttoning my shirt slowly, one button at a time, as if trying to make the moment last longer.

It's my favorite too, that brief period before you've seen everything, felt everything another person has to offer. How everything is so fragile, like the mood could get spoilt with one wrong move or word, and your body is a mess of hormones and adrenaline.

Soon though, she's done, and with a last tug on my sleeves, the shirt falls to the floor. She places her palm flat onto my chest, then curls her fingers, running her nails over my skin. Exquisite, slow, torture.

I close my eyes and thread my fingers through her

long hair, kissing her deeply, until her breaths pause along with my own. How sweet her lips taste, how fragrant her skin is. Both overwhelm me, and yet I fight with all I've got to maintain pace.

Her reactions suggest she likes it that way: slow.

Then, something about her changes, she pushes against me, guiding me backwards to the bed until I can go no further but down. She doesn't let up, and I find myself on my back, with her straddling me.

Her eyes are a soulful black which consume me, I can barely muster the discipline to look away. She pulls the dress over her head, revealing a red halter bikini, the straps of which had been teasing me with their presence all evening. Beautiful bronzed skin as far as the eye can see; almost spilling out of the tight confines of her top.

I reach out for her, grabbing her wrist and pulling her down against me. Her hair smells of flowers, her soft locks tickle me as they cascade over my bare chest and shoulders.

As I lie there, with this gorgeous voluptuous woman on top of me, kissing my chest, I can't help thinking that I've just made the most wonderful discovery. Like nobody has ever felt this way before. I certainly haven't. *Lust* I understand, and Mandi certainly inspires that in me as well, but all the other stuff is new. All evening I've felt this inexplicable drive to make her smile, to crack the surface and reach her core somehow.

The fact that she seemed so guarded made me even more determined.

This creature I see above me, staring down as she starts to unbutton my jeans is no longer out of reach though. She's present as present can be, and entirely focused on me as I am on her.

There's no pretence about her. No undeserved adulation, like I'd gotten from the waitress at the restaurant. No wonder Mandi had felt weird about it. There are two types of people in the world: leaders and followers. Mandi clearly is the former. Powerful and confident in herself, so she doesn't need to look to any outsider for direction

She lifts herself off me, letting me rid myself of the jeans at last. Meanwhile she reaches around and undoes the knots of her bikini top, revealing the rest of her exquisite body. Full-figured feminine perfection.

Some might mistake the dips and valleys of her flesh for flaws, but they're not. She's perfect just as she is. A Rubenesque goddess, who deserves my complete adoration.

Her eyes show not a hint of nerves, no doubts or concerns, like she's completely in tune with herself. It's a self-assurance that some with a lesser understanding of who she is might mistake for arrogance. I know better though.

ONLY A TASTE

We are one.

I lean up and wrap my arm around her, almost cradling her as I turn things upside-down. With her on her back, I'm free to reach over to retrieve the bag containing dessert. A selection of items, their sole purpose is to bring her pleasure.

"Close your eyes," I say.

She looks at me defiantly for just a moment before seemingly changing her mind and doing as I say.

Inside the bag, I'm spoilt for choice. Remembering her choice in gelato earlier today, I'd picked up some chocolate truffles with a hint of Cuban dark rum, rose-scented Turkish Delight as well as an old classic: chocolate covered strawberries. The fig and vanilla custard tart Chef Arnaud added on the house just because it's a new addition to his menu. Best to leave that for later, since it requires the use of a spoon and patience. Two things neither of us have right now.

I pick up a piece of Turkish Delight, careful not to spill any of the fine sugar onto the bed. The crinkle of the heavy paper bag seems to echo around the room.

"Open up," I whisper in Mandi's ear.

Her nose twitches, she's desperate to know what's coming. Soon though, she opens her mouth so I can feed her the treat. I dive down into her invitingly full cleavage, allowing myself a taste of her aroused nipple which had received a light dusting of sugar as I fed her.

She moans softly as she chews, encouraging me to stimulate her other breast with my hand.

I pause only to pick up another sweet, this one chosen blindly by touch. A truffle. I hold it between my teeth, offering it to her from my lips while slipping one hand between us for a first, most intimate touch. She arches upwards, gasping when I find her clit in between soft, inviting curls. I kiss her half-open lips, tempting me with the taste of rich chocolate.

With every bite I alternate the flavors I feed her, while continuing to lavish her body with affection, aiming to increase the intensity of her pleasure each time. It works, judging from her reactions, which have grown more pronounced after every mouthful.

Finally she can take it no longer, opening her eyes and focusing on the last truffle, which instead of feeding her, I finally deposit inside her belly button. I lick at it, tasting the bitter cocoa powder covering the lusciously rich chocolate inside.

Then I carefully pick it up with my teeth, and tickle her with its slightly bumpy texture, until it finally starts to melt against the heat of her skin. All the way down her lower abdomen I go, coming to a stop just above her mound. She leans up, her eyes wide with expectation and surprise as she observes me. I let go of the half-molten truffle, leaving it in her belly button again, then start to lick the trail of chocolate off her.

She writhes underneath me with every touch of my tongue. When she's clean, save for her bellybutton, I slip my fingers between her moist folds and into her at last, and just watch for a moment. She reacts sharply, crying out in pleasure. Her whole body moves under the gentle manipulations of my fingers, so I dive in for one last, chocolaty taste, taking my time on her bellybutton until no trace of truffle remains.

Finally her patience reaches its limits and she lifts herself until she can reach me. Her hands close around my cock, making me shudder with delight. It's almost too much, too intense. Just watching her enjoy herself brought me painfully close to my own release. It didn't help that I've been fighting these dark urges all evening, a primal lust so persistent I only barely managed to conceal it throughout our dinner date.

She looks me in the eye, no words are needed for me to know what she wants. It's not a pleading glance, but a command. Time for me to answer it.

I hurriedly find a condom in the drawer—this is one hotel I know to be well stocked at all times—and rush to put it on as she watches.

She spreads her beautifully voluptuous thighs, all the while continuing to hypnotize me with her eyes. The time for teasing is over, I couldn't do it even if I wanted to. I push into her, aiming to claim her just with that first move. Her lips open, but her moan sounds choked, as if she's trying to fight her release.

I am too, I don't want this first time to be over so soon.

But then she can't hold back any longer and starts to move underneath me. Her hips buck upwards, setting the pace she needs, and I follow along on her rhythm. I've picked up women before, and I've *fucked* plenty of them, but this... it's different. *She's different.* I hesitate to think of it as *making love*, but that's the only term that seems to fit.

Can you fall in love with someone you've only just met? This and many more confused thoughts enter my mind, before they are wiped out by the perfection of our union. The relentless rhythm she's chosen for us makes me blank out, until nothing matters anymore. Not the worry of whether she feels the same, not my curiosity at why tonight is so different than any other intimate encounter in my past.

She matters. Her eyes, which stare back at me, until they close involuntarily into a frown. Her soft feminine body, as it thrusts up at me every time I push deeply into her. Her gasps and moans that match my own.

She's *all* that matters.

I force myself back in control, but I'm desperately close to losing it. Her eyes are permanently shut now, and her moans quicken until there's almost no pause in between. I speed up along with her, feverishly focused on lasting long enough to take her over the edge. Then there's silence as she bites down hard on her bottom lip, and her body freezes underneath me. Every muscle of hers tightens, seemingly keen to keep me exactly where I am.

It's too much. Too intense. Too beautiful.

My own orgasm washes over me instantly. An explosion of energy originating deep inside my lower abdomen overwhelms me, until everything from my toes to my fingertips is filled with a mind numbing heat.

She opens her eyes, suddenly aware of what's happening, and starts to move again. I can't fight it, can't cooperate, I'm helplessly locked in place as she draws out our first release. Our moment of togetherness. Until we're both out of breath and paralyzed in exhaustion.

I force myself partially off her, struggling to make my muscles cooperate. Then I wrap my arm around her, and rest my head against hers. Her hair smells so nice, it intoxicates me all over again.

"Now I owe you two desserts," she says, her voice trailing off towards the end.

I smile, but the heavy feeling in my limbs and eyelids prevents me from responding.

After years of wandering, I feel like I've finally come home.

CHAPTER SEVEN

I lie awake, staring at the chandelier which glistens in the faintest beginnings of daylight filtering through the French windows. Beside me, Callum's deep, even breaths suggest he's still sleeping, so I take care not to move much so I don't disturb him.

There's a horrible, heavy feeling in my chest, like a weight holding me down under water. I'm drowning, desperate for air, but relief seems so impossibly out of reach, I don't know how to get it.

This has been the best night of my life, and with it, it's the worst. What if I just didn't go home today? What if I ran away with him; wouldn't that solve everything?

I know it would not. The guilt of leaving behind my family would eat me up.

But don't I deserve to be happy too? Do I have to do without, just so Mom and Dad can be proud of who I am? Even if it is a lie? Why does it have to be one or the other?

I turn onto my side, facing Callum's sleeping form. He looks so peaceful, like an angel—as stupid as that sounds. At dinner, he insisted I keep an open mind tonight, suggesting he's after something more than just a one-nighter. Could this beautiful man actually be *that* interested in me? He's successful, famous even, whereas I'm a failure professionally and not even a nice person most of the time. Sarcastic: definitely. Nice: not so much.

Neither am I that special to look at. I'm the girl who's been told her entire life that she'd be *so* pretty if only she lost a few pounds.

And then there's the baggage: not just one or two issues, but a whole collection the size and shape of a conservative extended family.

Whatever this is between Callum and me, it can't work out. There's no happy ending to be found here. And he couldn't possibly be wishing for one either.

Tears sting in my eyes, and I'm annoyed at myself for letting it get so far. Sarah was right: this was supposed to be my farewell party. A last celebration before I'd have to forget myself and fit in with whatever is expected of me. It was never meant to be a beginning of anything, just an ending.

I didn't think this could happen; that I'd go to bed with someone and get tangled up in complicated emotions afterwards. It certainly never happened to be me before. But for some reason now that I'm here, looking at him, I'm not thinking of escaping before he wakes up, or whether I'll need to block his number if he calls me too often afterwards.

It's the opposite. I wonder how long I can stay

here with him, before real life catches up with me. I'm terrified that he won't *want* to call. All the while, I have nothing to offer him at all.

The more I think about it, the more certain I am about what I must do. I need to be really clear with him, tell him that as nice as our time together has been, this is it. The end. Tonight will become a nice memory for us to keep, perhaps to think back to as *that crazy night in Brighton.* Nothing more.

It hurts to look at him now, knowing I'll probably never see him again after this, except on the damn TV. I lie back down on my pillow and cover my eyes with the back of my hand, doing everything possible to swallow my tears.

What the hell? I've never been the emotional type, why start now?

He's just a guy. We just had sex. No big deal. So why is my heart trying to make it into something more meaningful?

"Morning, beautiful."Callum's voice pierces through the silence. "You're up early."

"How did you know I was?" I ask, hoping my voice doesn't betray my innermost feelings.

"Your breathing. You sounded different when you were asleep."

It's time. The moment of truth. I have to tell him now, before he manages to distract me with his boyishly handsome looks and ruffled bed hair. Before he says something to make me reconsider.

I lean up on my elbows and look over at him. *Shit.* Just seeing his half-naked form as he sits up, ready to get out of bed, is making my heart beat faster again. I don't know if I can do this! If only I had another choice...

"I had a lovely time last night..." I start.

He turns, his blue eyes piercing me and peeling back my defenses layer by layer. "Me too."

"But..." Even my voice sounds breathless now, that's how uncharacteristically nervous I am.

"But things are very complicated right now and you're not looking for anything," he repeats my words from last night almost verbatim.

I press my lips together, again fighting the sting of tears and nod.

His expression is no longer carefree, but has hardened as he continues to look back at me. I wonder what he's thinking. I wonder if I really want to know.

"Look, it's not you, okay," I try to justify myself. "Things at home... My parents are very traditional."

"I see."

"They'll never let me date, especially not outside our community."

"How old are you again?"

I bite my tongue. He'll never understand. I'm not even sure *I* understand. It's so unfair that I have to choose between their happiness and my own. But crying about it isn't going to change anything.

"I really like you, Callum. I wish things were different."

"So do I." He turns around again, leaning forward to pick up his clothes off the floor.

There's nothing more to say, so I just watch him as he gathers his things and heads to the bathroom. The door shuts behind him with a painfully loud click. I fall back into my pillow, and focus on deep, even breaths. *Stay calm. This awful moment will pass.*

I stay like that for about five minutes, until the bathroom door opens again, revealing a fully dressed Callum. If it wasn't for the slight stubble on his chin—which could be justified as fashion—nobody could tell this overnight stay was unplanned.

"I have to get back into London for a meeting this morning," he says, while picking up his wallet, phone, and other items still on the antique-looking chest of drawers opposite the bed. Then he turns to face me, his expression is firm, almost neutral, although his eyes still betray the fiery passion that had made last night so special.

One, two steps forward, and he's at my bedside. He leans down, his face just an inch from mine, sending my self-control into a tailspin.

"I've heard what you said, and I understand," he says, while running his forefinger over my chin.

ONLY A TASTE

The tickle of his breath against my lips is almost too much, forcing my eyes to flutter shut a few times while he speaks.

"But don't think I'll give up that easily. This isn't goodbye." He emphasizes his statement with a kiss that knocks the wind out of me, then lets go and leaves me panting in bed as he makes his exit.

"Just leave the key in the room whenever you're done, it's all paid for. See you later, Mandi." The door clicks into place behind him, and the silence that remains overwhelms me.

After what feels like forever, I finally lean up and retrieve my phone from the bedside table and dial.

"Hey," Sarah's groggy voice answers. "What time is it?"

"Dunno. Hey, can you come and get me whenever you're ready? I'll text you the location," I say, doing my utmost to disguise the disillusionment in my tone.

There's a pause, and something sounding like a yawn on the other end. "Dude, you have to tell me all about last night, how was it? I'm assuming the date went well since I didn't hear from you..."

"Get ready, come pick me up, I'll tell you all about it on the drive home." I hang up before she has the chance to say anything else. Hopefully by the time we get together, I won't feel so raw and vulnerable. I'll tell Sarah what she wants to know, minus his identity and the part where I wished he wouldn't leave me behind. Even after I explicitly told him to.

This is all an impossible dream, isn't it? He can't be serious about planning to pursue me, after everything I tried to tell him? He can't possibly!

And yet, against my better judgment, I desperately hope to see Callum Byrne again.

CHAPTER EIGHT

"I'm home!" I announce myself as I close the front door of the house I grew up in behind me. It's four minutes past three. Not a bad time, considering we only got back from Brighton at eleven.

Bye, bye, outside world. You shall be missed.

"Mandeep!" Dadi—Dad's mom, who has lived with us for as long as I can recall—appears in the doorway leading to the living room, shuffling in my direction as quickly as she can manage with the help of her walking stick.

I put my bags down and rush towards her, giving her a warm hug. She's the one I missed the most when I moved away for college and it's so good to see her now that I'm back.

"Look at you! So skinny. Have you been eating properly?" She scrutinizes me up and down and pinches my cheek with her trembling fingers.

She looks frailer than when I last saw her and everyone else at my graduation ceremony. The lines on her face seem to have deepened, and her skin seems just that little bit more fragile than before. I should have visited, but the job hunt had taken up so much of my time, I didn't get the chance to.

"Don't worry, I've been taking care of myself."

"If you say so. You're just skin and bones, girl!" The quasi-strict expression on her face makes me smile and I hug her again. Even if she's obviously lying. Skin and bones; hah!

"Where is everyone?" I ask, upon letting her go again.

"The shop, of course. Where they always are."

Of course. It's the weekend, the busiest time of the week for a takeaway restaurant. Dad will be manning the phone, while Mom's in the kitchen, supervising the cooks. And ever since my little brother Jai got his license, he's been doing the deliveries.

I drag my two suitcases of clothes further into the hallway and dump them by the stairs. Sarah will drop the rest of the stuff in her car next weekend.

"Have you had lunch? Come eat something," Dadi waves at me as she turns to head back into the dining room.

"I had something on the way. Just going to put my stuff in my room, then I'm coming," I call after her.

Nothing has changed I see. Food still is the main social glue holding this family together. But before I feel like eating anything at all, I need a moment to myself to find my bearings.

I carry both my suitcases up to my old room. Everything, from the purple organza curtains, to the Moroccan style steel and glass lampshade, are a throwback to another era, one I don't belong to anymore. It's overwhelming, looking at it all. But it isn't nostalgia that hits me; it's despair.

Fighting back tears, I take a deep breath. If I'm going to stay here, things are going to have to change. I'll start with the bookcase full of old textbooks. What am I, back in school?

I dump one of my suitcases, the bigger pink one, onto the bed and start rummaging through the clothes I'd packed. All of it goes straight into the closet, without much thought. Make-up goes onto the dresser, underwear and socks into the drawer.

All the old junk I left behind when I moved out years ago, I simply brush aside. I'll sort it out later.

When I take my toiletry bag into the family bathroom across the hall, I realize that I've left my toothbrush and deodorant behind at Sarah's. Brilliant. I'll have to head to the shops as soon as possible.

By the time everything is sort of unpacked and I'm back downstairs, I'm exhausted, physically as well as mentally.

"I've made you some tea." Dadi points at the cup on the heavy wooden dining table in front of her, covered with an up-side-down saucer to keep it hot. "Sit, girl, you must be tired."

She slides a tray towards me featuring multiple bowls of nibbles, peanuts and other spicy treats. My stomach growls at the sight of it. I gratefully serve myself as I take a first sip of the strong, milky tea she's made. Nobody makes *chai* like Dadi does.

Sitting back in the chair, I close my eyes and try to relax.

"Thanks. It's been a long day," I mumble. Mainly it's the long night with little sleep leading up to today that's having an effect on me, but I keep that detail to myself.

She smiles at me, but doesn't say a word. There's always something in the way she looks at me that suggests she knows exactly what's going on in my head. Often, that has been reassuring. To feel understood by at least one person at home.But today, I can't help feeling uneasy about it.

What if she guesses what I was up to yesterday? I had a shower before setting off, and I'm obviously no longer wearing the same bikini and summer dress anymore. But, I can't help wondering if she has an inkling that I've been with a man last night. Glimpses of our escapades keep coming back to me when I least expect them to. What if it's written on my face?

"Your father tells me Mr. Gupta is very eager for you to start work," she says at last.

Mr. Gupta. Ugh. He and Dad have been friends for as long as we've lived in this neighborhood— pretty much forever. Of course he was happy to offer me a job. My inner cynic wants to believe it's because I'll be so ridiculously overqualified for it, that we're doing *him* a favor. In truth, I think it's going to be torture.

But, everyone has to start at the bottom, as Dad likes to say. I just never thought my completed degree would have me heading for a bookkeeping job where my main activity would consist of data entry for a shop selling cheap underwear imported from China.

"Yeah, I'm so excited too," I respond, while taking another sip of hot tea in an attempt to drown out the continuing sense of loss that's been hanging over me ever since I left Sarah this morning.

"You'll find something else in a while. You're smart, I've always said that you're smart. Give it a few months at least, though," Dadi tries to reassure me.

I smile bleakly at her, grateful she's latching on to my job concerns as the main source of my mood today. I'd feel horrible if she thought I was sad to be back home with her. And if she found out about Callum, well that's just a whole other bucketful of awkward right there.

We sit quietly while I finish my tea. Remembering my missing toiletries, I ask Dadi if we need anything else from the shops, to which she responds with a smile and a nod. I know exactly what she's after.

"Oh, Mandeep," Dadi reaches for my arm just as I'm about to leave and gives me a serious look. "As usual, no need to mention the gin to your father."

I wink at her. Our understanding still stands. "Of

course not. No need to mention to him that I'm not looking forward to the new job either."

"My lips are sealed, child. See you later."

I grab my handbag and I'm out the door.

The shopping centre is only a short walk away, and the blue, cloudless skies overhead suggest I'm safe to leave without an umbrella. While I'm already out, I might as well show my face at the takeaway too, give the impression that I'm happy to be back, etcetera.

The warm summer air carries with it the heavy floral scents of our neighbor's, Mrs. Singh's, colorful front garden. Other neighbors must have been mowing their lawns, adding the aroma of cut grass as their contribution to today's summery atmosphere.

The contrast between yesterday and today couldn't be bigger. From the city, followed by the hustle and bustle of Brighton beach, I'm back in suburbia. Back in our old street, where I know every single person who lives here—mainly because nobody ever seems to move away—and more unnervingly, everyone knows me too.

"Mandi!" a voice drags me out of my bittersweet thoughts. "So it's true, you're back."

I look up to find Leila from five houses down standing there looking down her nose at me with her arms propped up against her hips.

A casual bystander may have mistaken her smile for genuine, but I know better. Leila is the mean girl of the neighborhood after all.

"Leila. Nice to see you," I remark, returning a fake grin of my own. *With neighbors like her, who needs enemies?*

"Your parents must be thrilled."

"I'm sure they are."

She stands in silence for a moment while really looking me up and down. As if she's tallying up new ways to insult me. A few years ago, I would have felt embarrassed; even humiliated. But now, it's just irritating. I have bigger fish to fry.

"So I hear Mr. Gupta has a job lined up for you," she says finally. "Exciting. You know, I applied for that one too, but I guess he owed your dad, or something." As if she needed even more reason to hate me, now she thinks I stole her job away from her too. Great.

"Just chance, I'm sure."

"Yeah..." She pauses for a few awkward seconds. "Well anyway, good luck with that."

"Thanks. See you around." I shoot one last glance in her direction, only to find she's whipped her phone out of her pocket already to spread the news that I'm back. I roll my eyes and wonder how many more uncomfortable conversations with people from my past lie ahead...

Thankfully the rest of the walk, as well as my short visit to the small supermarket across from our takeaway, passes without further interruptions. The bored-looking middle-aged bleached blonde with the dangerously long red fingernails scans my meager purchases—toothbrush, deodorant, bottle of gin—without comment. Thank God I don't know her, or she'd no doubt start grilling me about the booze.

Shit, the takeaway! I can't very well walk in there carrying a bottle of gin!

"Umm, sorry, mind if I leave this here for just a minute? I'll be right back," I ask, pointing at the bag.

She nods in such a disinterested manner, I wonder if she's even heard me properly, but breathe a sigh of relief when she accepts it when I hand her my shopping across the counter.

Moments later, I cross the threshold of *'Passage to India'*, which has looked and smelled exactly like it has done for the past twenty years at least. The aroma of mixed spices brings back a whole lot of memories.

"Dad, I'm back!" I call out at the empty wooden counter. Dad appears from the back within seconds, a wide smile on his face.

"Good. Your mother is in the kitchen," he says, before turning around "Kamal, come out here for a moment?"

"What is it?" Mom shouts back, before popping her head around the doorway. "Mandeep! Sweetheart!" She rushes towards me and gives me an awkward hug, trying not to touch her flour-covered hands on my clothes. "How lovely that you're back. Did you go home yet? Of course you did, you wouldn't have just come straight here, would you?"

"I've left my stuff in my room. Just needed a few toiletries," I explain.

"Right... Right..." She takes a step back and smiles at me for a moment. "It's so wonderful you've come. Finally the family is complete again. Now everything can get back to normal."

"Yes. Wonderful," I repeat. "Well I just popped in to say hello, but I'm kind of tired after lugging my suitcases around on and off the train, so perhaps I'll rest a bit. See you at night?"

"Sure thing, darling." Mom gives me a wave and turns to head back into the kitchen.

"Bye, Mandeep," Dad says.

I wave back at them and head across the street again to collect my shopping. While it's nice to see everyone again, I can't help feeling just a little bit resentful.

I'm back. And now I'm stuck here.

CHAPTER NINE: CALLUM

"So if you're keeping the lamb as a main, you'll have to rethink the starters. It doesn't gel together," Jack Cleary remarks, while looking up from the print-out with suggested dishes.

"Right you are," I say, though I'm only half listening to him.

"Also, you're quite thin on salads. That may fly for a winter menu, but in the summer, you're going to turn people off, son." Jack leans out of his leather armchair and picks up his scotch, clinking the ice in it together while he brings it to his lips.

"Mhm."

"Well that does it. Why so distracted? Are my insights boring you?" He gives me a strict stare, just like back in the day when I was training under him. He's always had an air of authority about him; ruling his kitchen with an iron fist.

"It's not that, I'm just finding it hard to concentrate. Didn't sleep well."

"I recall a time when you didn't need a mundane thing such as sleep."

"Well we're not getting any younger, are we?" I attempt a joke, but it falls on deaf ears. What am I saying; Jack has at least ten years on me.

"There's more to it than that. I'd be willing to put money on it," Jack says. "This isn't so much a sleep issue as a... It's a woman, isn't it?"

I sit back into the creaky leather and let my thoughts wander back to Brighton. Back to Mandi.

"That obvious, is it?" I ask, while picking up my own glass for a sip.

The Scotch is smooth. Expensive. Exactly to Jack's taste. It's quite early in the day to be drinking, but I decide that I don't care.

"In some cultures—say in Hull—our friendship would be old enough to have children of its own. Of course, it's bloody obvious."

I let out a chuckle. He's right. We've known each other coming up to fifteen—maybe sixteen years now, when I first joined his restaurant as a fresh-faced dishwasher with grand ambitions.

"Fine. It's a woman."

"Well don't be so mysterious!"

I take a deep breath, sighing all the air back out again. Where to begin...

"I may not have found the perfect location for my Brighton restaurant, but I did find something else there."

"Oh?" Jack folds his hands together, waiting for me to continue.

"Her name is Mandi, and she's..." *Beautiful,*

magnificent, perfect in every way. "Probably unavailable."

"That's never stopped you before," Jack remarks.

"It's not so simple. There are family issues."

"Well you certainly work quickly if you already know all about her family. You were only in Brighton for a day, weren't you?"

"One night."

"One night..." he sounds thoughtful. "So, tell me more."

"We both ordered the same flavor gelato, but they only had one scoop left."

He laughs out loud. "That sounds like the beginning of a girly movie."

It does, he's right, but I'm in no mood to laugh about it. "Then I asked her to dinner, and that was that."

"That's all the detail I'm going to get out of you, isn't it?" he teases.

"Use your imagination, you old pervert."

I take another sip, savoring the burn of the Scotch on my tongue. I've got to get in touch with her.

"Hey, Callum," a cheerful voice greets me from behind. I turn to find Carrie, Jack's assistant, standing in the doorway, waving at me. "I thought I heard your voice in here. How's it going?"

I exchange a quick look with Jack, who looks thoroughly amused. Carrie has always had a thing for me, and there have been times—one time—she managed to tempt me into something more than just idle small talk. She has nothing on Mandi though. I don't know what I was thinking.

"Just working on my new menu. In fact, we ought to get back to that, if you don't mind." I shoot Carrie a quick business-like nod and turn to face Jack who still has a smug smile plastered on his face.

"No problem, you boys get back to it," she says, presumably while leaving.

"I see. You're thoroughly screwed, mate," Jack remarks.

"Bugger off. Now what were you saying about the lamb and the starters?"

***

By late afternoon, Jack and I finally manage to put something together we're both reasonably happy with. A menu with something for everyone, which won't tax the kitchen too much even during the busy periods. Perfect for a new restaurant. We can always switch things up once the staff are properly settled in.

After saying our goodbyes, I find myself wandering through Waterloo Station on my own. As insanely busy and chaotic a place it is, somehow walking through the crowds alone has a calming effect on me. The ambient noise of a thousand people rushing through the main hall and to and from platforms, is almost hypnotic. Whenever I have something to mull over, this is where my feet seem to take me.

What do I know about Mandi?

The quick glance I managed to steal at the expired student ID card in her wallet gave me her full name: Mandeep Grewal. I know her parents live in Langley, and she's just moving back in with them. How many Grewal families who run a takeaway could there be in Langley? It's not that big of a place, is it?

Although she insisted that we have no future together because her folks would disapprove, I know I can't just let this go. I meant it when I told her this morning wasn't goodbye. Within just a few hours, she's embedded herself in my thoughts permanently.

When I close my eyes, I can still see her smile; her eyes full of warmth when she lets her guard down. I can still smell her sweet scent and imagine the taste of her lips against mine.

I've had relationships before, though arguably not many serious ones, but this connection I felt with her was unlike anything I'd experienced with anyone else. It's all new, yet I instinctively know it's not a fad that will just pass in time.

I decide to head home to think things over and perhaps do a bit of research on her. Perhaps I can find out more about her family, or look her up online somehow.

ONLY A TASTE

Of course I could just call the number she gave me, but what if she doesn't answer? When she gave me her number, it was before we'd even talked properly. What if it's not actually hers? What if her plan was always to ditch me, so she purposefully gave out a fake number to avoid complications?

In this day and age, you can find a person's whole life on the internet. In case the number turns out to be a fake, there has got to be a way I can get in touch with her. Otherwise I might have to resort to going door-to-door in Langley until I find the right house.

That would make things a lot more awkward than they need to be. But I'll do it if I have to. She's worth it.

"Excuse me?" a voice interrupts.

"Yes?" I respond, almost on autopilot. The expression on the professional-looking woman in the trouser suit is one I know all too well. She's recognized me.

"Are you...?"

"The one."

"Would you be able to..."

"Sign that?" I ask, pointing at the magazine she's holding with my face on the cover. "Sure."

She smiles gratefully while I go through the motions of giving her my autograph. This sort of thing happens so often, I'm well beyond thinking about it. But Mandi... it was weird for her last night with the waitress. Could she ever get used to this?

What if I find her? What if her supposed family issues aren't that big of a deal after all, but she can't deal with the constant spotlight on my life; and by extension on hers? Now I'm really getting ahead of myself.

I nod at the woman, shake her hand, and leave her standing in the middle of the crowds in Waterloo's main hall, clutching onto her newly signed magazine. I head out into the street with the beginnings of a plan developing in my head. First, I'll try to find Mandi online. Then we'll see what happens.

"Taxi!" I wave at a black cab approaching from the left.

"Where to?" the cabbie asks.

I give him my home address and gaze out the window at the world passing us by. As soon as I get home, I'll see if I can get in touch with her somehow. I owe it to us both to at least try.

I reach my place fifteen minutes later, and I'm still determined. Ignoring the long To Do list on the notepad on the coffee table, I open my laptop instead, and start searching for Mandi. It seems she shares her name with thousands of others, so I change strategy and search for more details on the takeaway in Langley instead.

Bingo.

Old articles pop up about her and her family, the

sort of quaint news you get in local papers. *Local takeaway wins Best Curry of Slough award.* A short quote from Mr. Grewal, presumably her dad, in a longer article about the redevelopment of a park. *Langley girl comes second in Craft Fair competition;* that sort of thing.

The photograph with the latter article catches my attention instantly. It's her, a few years younger of course, and at the same time so very different. The hip length hair worn in a thick braid made her look a lot more ethnic than she does now. But the sparkle in her eyes and smile are unmistakably her own.

An hour passes as I continue my stalkerish behavior. None of what I find reveals a subtler way of contacting her, though. I'm going to have to rely on the phone number she gave me yesterday. I guess I'll find out soon enough whether it works.

I hover over the 'call' button for a while, then put my phone back down in my lap again. Too soon. I'm going to give it at least another day or so.

As if by magic, my phone starts ringing in my hand. Unlisted number.

"Hello?" I answer, dreading as well as hoping Mandi was having the exact same thoughts as me and actually made the call herself.

"Callum, it's Trisha. You have a moment?"

I close my eyes and breathe a sigh of relief or disappointment; I'm not sure which. Trisha is the new PR contact for the TV network that airs my show.

"Yeah, sure, what's going on?"

"We're going to push the new season hard. Media appearances, interviews, the whole lot," she says

"Go on..." I grab my notepad and pen from the table and settle back into my chair while she runs me through the various promotional events she wants me to do. Looks like I have a busy few weeks ahead of me.

CHAPTER TEN

I start my job with Mr. Gupta sharp at nine on Monday morning. Although the first day is intense because I don't know what I'm doing yet, it soon turns into the drudgery I expected it to be. Tuesday, Wednesday and even Thursday pass without incident or excitement. I go to work in the morning, and try to survive the day without having any existential crises. In the evenings I head home to help out with dinner while trying not to think too much.

It's only at night, and during those moments before fully waking up early in the morning, that Callum stalks my thoughts. And boy, is it hard to banish those dreams from my imagination for the rest of the day.

My approach to fitting in back at home almost works, until finally on Friday evening, I arrive home to quite the spectacle in our living room.

Mom, Dad, Dadi and even Jai are dressed as if they're about to attend a wedding. Opposite them on the other sofa, there's another set of well-polished parents and a guy, who looks completely and utterly terrified.

"Mandeep, come sit with us. We'd like you to meet the Sandhus."

My heart sinks. Considering I've never seen these people before, and the state the guy—roughly my age—is in, this can only mean one thing: our parents have collectively decided to play matchmaker. *Fuck*.

In an effort to hide my annoyance, I bow my head and mumble a greeting at the visitors, before sitting down next to Dadi with my hands folded and my eyes fixed straight ahead.

"So lovely to meet you. What a lovely girl," the woman—Mrs. Sandhu—remarks, while exchanging an approving look with her husband. Their son barely even looks up from the floor.

"She's just completed her Bachelor's in Business Administration," my dad says proudly.

"Very bright. And she cooks well too," Mom adds.

I can hear Jai chuckle under his breath, but sadly he's too far away for me to kick in the shin. *Just you wait 'til it's your turn, dipshit.*

" So, what does your son do?" Dad asks.

"Oh, Diljeet is working with a multinational in the city. He's just been promoted to team leader," Mr. Sandhu beams.

Next thing I know, our parents are comparing salaries, both current as well as projected. I wish for the ground to just open up and swallow me whole.

"Anyway, what do you say we let the kids get to know each other a little? How about a drink, Mr. Sandhu?" Dad suggests, gesturing at me to get up and take the Sandhus' man-child somewhere for a private chat. As if this meeting couldn't get any worse.

I sigh, then head for the kitchen area to pick up a

bottle of Coke and two glasses. Then, out the door and into the hallway and up the stairs I go. Diljeet is a whole bunch of steps back. I can hear his folks encouraging him behind me.

I don't even check what he's doing behind me, it's enough that I hear footsteps.

"Want some?" I ask once inside my room, holding up a glass with my back still turned to him.

"Uhh... Sure." He clears his throat, but is unable to disguise the nerves in his voice.

I pour two glasses, then turn, handing him his. He doesn't even look directly at me.

"So... I guess we're supposed to get to know each other," I say, while checking the clock above my old desk. Five minutes alone with this guy would be too long, but I don't think I could get away with less.

"Yeah..."

Silence.

I look at him, as he stares at his shoes. I bet he's a virgin.

"So?"

"So?" he repeats.

"Who are you?"

"Diljeet. From Staines."

I decide to give him a chance to continue this very meaningful exchange, but he's not exactly a sparkling conversationalist. In fact, now he's quiet again. Without my intervention, the silence lasts a whole minute. I know this because I'm timing it on the wall clock.

"So have your parents met with a lot of girls yet?"

I ask at last.

If brown skin could blush properly, he'd be red by now. He shakes his head.

"How do you think it's going so far?"

He shrugs. *Yeah. Whatever.*

"Whenever you're done, let's go back inside before they wonder what we're up to." I put my empty glass down on the desk and head straight for the door without giving him the chance to reply.

Once I make it back inside the living room, Jai can barely contain his amusement, much to Mom and Dad's displeasure. Dadi gives me a look of understanding and pats on the sofa beside her.

"Well?" Mom asks, though I instinctively realize it's a rhetorical question.

"It's been wonderful meeting you, Mr. and Mrs. Sandhu. And Diljeet, of course." Dad nods at the lot of them, just as *His Shyness* shuts the living room door behind him, looking even more terrified than he did when we were alone in my room. "We'll be in touch."

As his parents get up to say their goodbyes to my parents, I don't have the energy to keep up appearances anymore. All I can do is sit next to Dadi, who is gently patting the top of my hand as if to tell me everything is going to be all right.

The second everyone makes it out the front door, and Mom and Dad come back into the lounge, they both pounce.

"He's a handsome boy, isn't he?" Mom asks.

"Very well settled. Good family," Dad adds.

"I'll be in my room," I say, and bolt out the door

and up the stairs. What the actual fuck? They couldn't wait at least a week to let me get used to being back home before parading me around like cattle at an auction? Well settled, bah! I slam my door and turn the key.

"Hey, Mandi," Jai's voice filters through my bedroom door moments later. "Awesome guy, innit?"

"Leave me alone!" I shout.

He bursts out laughing on the other side, requiring me to turn on the radio to drown him out. The irritating little shit can drop dead for all I care.

It's at that moment, to the raw and vulnerable vocals of Tom Odell's *Another Love* that the first tears start to form. If I stand my ground, I can probably steer my folks in the direction of someone a bit more compatible, but what would be the point? I already know nobody could ever match up to Callum!

Being honest with my folks just isn't going to work either. If they found out about Callum at all, they'd just dig in further about Diljeet or whoever else comes along. They'd never let me date on my own; and certainly not a white guy.

On top of that, I don't even know if Callum is even interested at all. We haven't been in touch since that one night, obviously. Perhaps he's been a lot more successful forgetting me, than I have been at forgetting him.

It's hopeless. All of it.

I hide my face in my pillow and let the floodgates open until my pillowcase is soaked with tears. There's no way out of this. Either I take a stand for me, *my happiness*, and destroy theirs in the process, or I need to accept the fact that I just cannot get what I so desperately want.

"Mandeep?" Dadi's voice calls out from beyond my door, followed by a subtle knock.

I sniffle loudly, hoping to contain all the wetness and goo that is still dripping from several of my facial orifices.

"Open up, talk to me."

Pressing the pillow on my face one final time in the hopes it'll dry me off a bit, I drag myself up and open the door.

"Yes, Dadi?" I whimper a bit too miserably.

"Child, tell me what's wrong." She shuffles inside, then closes the door behind her, almost dropping her walking stick in the process.

I sit back down on the bed with my hands folded and wait for her to reach me. She puts her hand on my shoulder, squeezing it encouragingly.

"I wasn't impressed either, I'll have you know," she says, before sitting down with a loud sigh.

Her remark makes me smile despite myself, but the tears are still coming, just more silently than before.

"I... He... Oh God, what do I do?" I complain.

"Your father is a very stubborn man, has been ever since he was little."

"Yeah..."

"I remember when he was eight years old, some older boys from the neighborhood told him he was too little to play football with them. And he played and played on his own, every day after school, practicing so that he would be good enough. It was so hot outside that he fainted. We had to take him to the doctor because he'd gotten dehydrated. Still, he refused to give up and just went back to practicing as soon as I let him out of my sights. That's how stubborn your father was."

This story, which I've heard probably a hundred times before, does nothing to make me feel better. If anything, it's further proof that everything is lost. I hide my face in my hands.

"How many times can I say 'no' before Dad loses patience, you think?" I ask, hoping that if I can get away with refusing a whole bunch of matches, perhaps someone or other will come along who will make me reconsider everything. Someone I could actually accept. Though I doubt that's even possible.

"You know when I was to marry your grandfather, I wasn't thrilled either. Back in those days, you didn't even meet until the day of the wedding. I thought he was too skinny, too awkward when I first saw him at the ceremony. But in time, I grew to love him. That's what happens in arranged marriages. The start is never easy, even if you think you know each other well. Marriage is never easy." She looks down at her hands, gripping the knob on her stick tightly.

"Mhm," I respond, lacking the words for a proper reply.

A strange, extra quiet silence follows.

"Who is he?" Dadi's words cut through my defenses like a hot knife through butter.

I look up, shocked at her question. *Did I hear that right?*

"What?" I ask.

"Don't you play with me, young lady. I wasn't born yesterday."

I sigh and lie back on the bed, covering my eyes with my arm.

"Just. A guy." Just the most amazing guy I've ever met, who's always in the back of my mind, no matter how hard I try to forget him.

"And? Is he ready to marry you?" she asks.

"No! It's... I don't know. We haven't talked about it." He couldn't possibly be. He doesn't seem the type anyway, plus we haven't spoken. What do I even know about him? Practically nothing. For all I know he's gone straight from me to someone else, without looking back even once.

"I suggest that you do, before your father gets in one of his moods and puts his foot down." She pats my leg, then heaves herself up with the help of her stick and shuffles back to the door.

"Consider it. If you can get this boy to meet your father, perhaps something can be done."

I'm still in shock that she could see through me so easily, when the door clicks back into place behind her. Of course there's no way I could ever consider her advice. Despite his insistence that last week's one-nighter was more than that, he hasn't been in touch.

And Dadi doesn't know he's white, or she wouldn't even have suggested any of this.

From the corner of my eye I notice that the little

light in the top corner of my phone is blinking. I must have forgotten it on silent when I left work earlier. Perhaps it's Sarah. I could use a good talk with her right now; or rather, a good cry.

I unlock the screen and find that it's not Sarah at all. It's a message from Callum. I open it with shaky fingers.

This is a sign, isn't it? After wondering whether he even thinks about me at all? It's as if he could read my mind and knew I'm in trouble.

'Mandi. Sorry I've not been in touch, work has been crazy this past week. I really would like to see you again though, can't stop thinking about you. Call me when you can? Callum'

After reading and re-reading the message a few times, I decide not to call. Not that I don't appreciate him reaching out, I just wouldn't know what to say, plus I'm all stuffed up after crying earlier. The last thing I want right now is to have to explain why. Instead, I type out a quick response:

'Been thinking about you too, but things are really complicated at home right now. I'll call you tomorrow. Mandi'

The moment I've hit 'send', I pull up Sarah's number instead.

CHAPTER ELEVEN

After being plagued by confusing as well as explicit dreams featuring one—and only one—perfect subject all night, Saturday morning has crept up on me rather suddenly. I rush to get up, splash water on my face and head for the stairs. Sarah is coming in a short while with the rest of my stuff, and it would be nice to at least be showered and ready beforehand.

After living together for years, it's been weird not having her around at all. It's only been a week, but I've really missed her.

As is typical for weekends in our house, everyone else has been up for hours when I make it downstairs at ten. The living/dining areas are abuzz with activity. Dadi is sitting in her usual seat at the head of the table, with Dad towards her right. Mom, meanwhile, is rushing back and forth between the open plan kitchen and the table, bringing in breakfast.

Off in the lounge area, the large flat screen TV is on, but nobody seems to be paying attention to it.

"Mandi, finally, you're awake. Make some tea, will you?" Mom says, the moment she spies me standing in the doorway.

I suppress a yawn and start making myself useful.

Cups. Kettle. Tea bags.

"Jai, what time is your game?" Dad asks. I turn around to observe the exchange.

Jai mumbles something about eleven, before stuffing way too much omelet into his mouth.

I turn back when the kettle's click lets me know the water is boiling and ready.

"Shush... My program is coming," Dadi says to no one in particular, while picking up the remote and dramatically increasing the volume.

Right in the middle of pouring the third and fourth cup, watching the near boiling water create swirls of dark brown originating from the tea bag, I hear something from the living area that stops me in my tracks. A familiar voice.

I accidentally spill some of the hot water over the counter, then quickly recover and put the kettle down to avoid further accidents. When I turn around, despite being as far away from the TV as I possibly could be, I instantly recognize Callum's handsome face.

Fuck. Of course. I had forgotten all about Dadi's love for a BBC weekend morning staple: 'Saturday Kitchen'. Next to the smiling host of the program, Callum is animatedly explaining something or other, but I can't seem to concentrate on his words.

This show. It's hosted live, isn't it? That means I'm literally looking at him in real-time. Almost as if he's literally standing here in our family living room!

"Mandeep? Oi!" Mom snaps her finger, startling me. "How about that tea? What's wrong with you? You look like you've seen a ghost."

"Tea. Of course." I turn around again, force a couple of deep breaths to get rid of the tightness in my chest, and pour hot water into the remaining cups. My hands still shake when I add milk and place the cups on a tray ready to deliver to the table.

"Perhaps she's just distracted because she can't stop thinking about Diljeet Sandhu," Jai remarks, chuckling to himself. "Mandi and Diljeet, sitting in a tree..."

"Shut up!" I shoot him a nasty look. The worst part is that he's hit the truth on the head without realizing, except it's Callum, not Diljeet, who's on my mind as well as on our bloody TV this morning. Must avoid looking at him. *Shit*. This is really bad.

"Are you okay, darling? You look pale," Mom asks again, touching my forehead with the back of her hand while I put the tea down.

"Yeah, fine. Had some trouble sleeping," I mumble, while making my way to the other side of the table. Even though I sit down with my back towards the TV, Callum's voice is still throwing me off balance.

To think he actually messaged me last night. And I said I'd call him! What the hell will I say? I like him, of course I do, but I have nothing whatsoever to offer him. He's not going to be content with the occasional phone call and message. I wouldn't be either, in his place.

I should ignore him. I should tell him to go away and delete my number. I should...

"Mandeep!" Dad almost shouts. His expression suggests he's been trying to get my attention for a bit too long already.

"Uhh... yes?"

"The salt."

I look over at the salt shaker right in front of my plate and almost knock it over while picking it up to hand it to Dad.

"She really doesn't look well. Are you sure you don't need to see a doctor?" Mom asks.

I just shake my head and start poking around in my food. Ugh. At this rate, I'm going to make all of them suspicious.

"Shh... I can't hear the TV," Dadi says, while increasing the volume yet again.

While everyone else is quietly eating, I rush to clean my plate as much as I can before excusing myself and heading back upstairs. That was bizarre. Let's hope Callum doesn't turn up in more unexpected places or I might just have a meltdown.

A quick shower later, the doorbell rings as I've just finished drying my hair. That'll be Sarah! And she couldn't have arrived at a better time.

I race downstairs, but Mom has beaten me to the door.

"Morning, Mrs. Grewal." Sarah shoots me a wide smile as she nods at Mom.

"Oh there you are, Mandi, your friend is here. Let me know if you need anything." She turns and heads back into the living area, giving us some much needed privacy.

"Oh my God, I'm so glad to see you," I say, while giving her a hug.

"Me too," she responds.

"How about we quickly unload your car and then head out somewhere for coffee?" I suggest. I can't wait to get out of here and tell her all about the mess I've found myself in. Yesterday's set-up orchestrated by my folks was awkward enough, but I think it's time to spill the beans about Callum. There's only so much confusion I can deal with on my own, and it would be good to get her insights before I call him and accidentally muck things up further.

She nods, then cocks her head to the side. "You look tired, are you okay? You're not getting sick, are you?"

"God, why does everyone keep asking me that this morning?" I complain.

"Because it's obvious."

I shake my head. "Later. Let's get this over with

first."

She shrugs and heads out towards her car while I follow. There are only about half a dozen boxes, so it doesn't take long for us to get everything out of her rust bucket vehicle and into my room.

I sit down on the bed and rub my eyes. I really am exhausted this morning.

"So, you want to tell me what's going on now?" Sarah asks.

After taking a moment to figure out where to start, I decide it's best not to beat around the bush.

"You know the guy I met in Brighton?" I begin.

"Yeah."

"He wants to keep in touch."

"So? Tell him to leave you alone." Sarah squints at me suspiciously, but then her eyes widen when she realizes what I'm trying to tell her. "Holy shit, you *like* him!"

I sigh. "Yeah. I do like him. It's a massive pain in my ass."

"So now what? Are you going to tell your parents?"

"My parents? They seem to be intent on marrying me off to whichever candidate has the best possible career prospects. It's like a bloody job interview. Whether I like the guy or not doesn't seem to be much of a priority." I let my shoulders hang down in defeat as I tell her in exacting detail about yesterday's post-work ambush and Diljeet Sandhu, the shy virgin.

"But, they're your *parents*! Surely they want you to be happy in life, don't they?" Sarah's shocked expression emphasizes that she hadn't taken much of what I'd told her about my background seriously.

"Of course they do, but they think that's what they're doing! They think in the long term that's what'll keep me happy," I explain. "I should just tell him to leave me alone, you're right." Just the thought hurts more than anticipated. I'm not sure I have the strength to do that.

"No! You can't! What if the both of you are totally right for one another? What if you're meant to be?"

I always knew Sarah was a romantic at heart, but what she's telling me now is next level. And unhelpful to boot.

"But what's the point, when my parents will never agree to let us be together?"

Sarah sighs deeply, then places her hand on top of mine. "I can't advise you about that. But there will come a time when you have to choose between your family and your own happiness."

Even though she can't fully relate to my situation, she's right about that. I will have to choose.

But perhaps, I just need some time to figure this thing out. Maybe my fascination with Callum is just a phase I'll grow out of. I should keep in touch with him behind everyone's back and see if things between us fizzle out naturally. And then, I won't have to tell a soul about it. Indeed, perhaps everything will find a way of working itself out.

"Anyway, how about that coffee?" Sarah asks.

I sigh deeply, reassured in the knowledge that now I have at least some semblance of a plan. Even if it relies almost completely on apathy.

"Yes. Let's go."

"I also have a bit of news I wanted to share with you, actually," Sarah tells me while we make our way out of my room and down the stairs.

"Oh yeah? Spill."

"Yeah, so, I got a job!" Sarah says.

"You already had a job." Unlike me.

She counters with a dismissive wave.

"Just freelancing; nothing stable. But this, this will be a *proper* job."

I grab my handbag on the way out of the house, then pat her on the shoulder with my free hand. "That's great, congratulations!"

"Yeah, so you remember that classmate of mine, Megan?" Sarah carries on.

"Uh-huh."

"She works for this website, *'Celeb Roundup'*, doing the lifestyle column. She put in a good word for me with her boss. I start in two weeks."

I frown. A gossip website? She sounds so excited though, bless her.

"It's actually perfect timing that we're meeting up this weekend, because I'm planning to move closer to the office to avoid the monster commute. I start house hunting next week!"

"Wow, this is all happening pretty quickly, huh?" I say, unsure what to think about all this. A couple of weeks back we were living in a tiny flat in the city together, and now I'm back home and even she's moving away. Things are changing a bit too quickly for my taste.

One thing is for sure, though. I was right to hide Callum's identity from her. She must never know who he is.

***

In the afternoon, after Sarah as well as mostly everyone else has left the house, I'm back in my room to try and build myself up for that all important first phone call.

It's strange, how we've done so many things in person, and yet simply dialing Callum's number to talk to him seems like such a big step. What if I'm interrupting something? What if he's busy?

Only one way to find out.

I dial his number before I get the chance to chicken out. It rings once, twice, thrice, and then he picks up.

"Mandi, hi!" He sounds genuinely pleased to hear from me, which helps some ways towards making me less nervous.

"Callum. How are you?" I ask.

"Not bad, but busy. If trying to open a new restaurant wasn't enough, now the network is after my life to promote the new season of my show as well. I just did a promo appearance this morning, actually."

I'm reminded of the sheer awkwardness of having him pop up on our TV earlier today. I close my eyes and breathe deeply. It's good to hear his voice. Comforting.

"Oh yeah, I actually saw that. To my own detriment," I blurt out.

"Was it that bad?" he teases, making me chuckle.

I counter by telling him all about this morning, when I nearly spilled everyone's tea hearing his voice behind me. Thankfully this retold version actually is a lot funnier than how it felt when it happened, and we share a good laugh.

"... I almost had a heart attack," I chuckle.

"I must say I was a bit worried, messaging you last night," Callum remarks after a short pause.

"Why?"

"Call me paranoid, but part of me was convinced you'd given me a fake number."

"Is it?" I'm doing my best not to burst out

laughing, mainly because I almost did.

"Yeah... I think it was the 'I'm here with a friend, can she come too?' response to me asking you out that threw me."

"That seemed like a funny thing to say at the time," I remark dryly, to which he laughs again.

"Funny, yes. I guess I can see that."

Just like that, a couple of laughs and nonsensical exchanges later, things are fine again. I lie back on my bed, mobile phone in hand and close my eyes, just focusing on our conversation. It's almost like he's here with me, lying next to me. Of course if that were the case, we wouldn't be *just talking*.

CHAPTER TWELVE:
CALLUM

I haven't seen Mandi in weeks. The occasional phone conversation and back and forth messaging has been frightfully dissatisfying. She feels the same, or so I assume, based on how she tends to sound over the phone.

My decision to make the trip to Langley didn't actually involve her directly, though. She would have said no, and tried to dissuade me. But, her folks work pretty much constantly through the weekends and she told me that her grandmother has some neighborhood bingo event to go to today.

So, today is the perfect day to give Mandi a little surprise. And meeting in person will give us the chance to find out if whatever we feel for one another is real, or just a desperate yearning to get back the memories of that one perfect night together.

I pull into her street, and the SatNav confirms her house should be up ahead on the right. Number seven.

My heart is racing, and I run my hands through my hair in an attempt to calm my nerves. It doesn't work.

Why am I even nervous? She liked me, right? She could have told me to bugger off on the phone if she didn't want to keep in touch. Instead, we've been in touch daily since that first phone call. And most of the time, she's initiated it.

It occurs to me that coming here in my Aston Martin was quite dumb, though. People will see it and talk. I should have rented a car: something more normal like a modest hatchback.

I find a parking spot a little ways up the road, far enough from her house, and leave the car there. Hopefully this will be enough to divert suspicions.

Crap, I should have brought flowers. No, that would be hard to explain to her folks. Chocolates. I should have brought chocolates. *Damn.*

As I consider back and forth whether I'm making a huge mistake, I see the curtains of the house I'm parked in front of twitch. Nosy neighbors. Brilliant.

I quickly get out of the car and head for her place, while scanning the otherwise empty street. It seems to be a rather typical neighborhood. Terraced houses with perfectly manicured front gardens. Hatchback cars and station wagons in all shades of grey line the street.

What am I going to say to her? What if she's upset that I came here?

I decide to just go for it. It's too late to back out now.

ONLY A TASTE

I ring the bell and almost instantly come face-to-face with what looks like a younger, male version of Mandi. Their eyes are the same color, the same shape even. His face resembles hers quite a lot, except for the carefully trimmed edging of beard, and the ultra-short buzz cut you often see on youths living in the inner city.

"Yeah?" the guy, presumably Mandi's brother, says. "Who are you?"

"Is Mandi home?" I ask.

He scrutinizes me for a moment, then pauses in the doorway, as if he's still deciding what to do.

"Jai, who is it? Is it a courier? I'm expecting a parcel," Mandi's voice calls out from inside the house.

"I dunno, he don't look like a courier," Jai shouts back.

Footsteps come down the stairs, until she appears in the hall behind her brother. Breathtaking. Even simple jeans and a fitted plain black t-shirt can make her look radiant somehow.

"Oh shit," she blurts out.

Well, this is awkward.

"Hi, Mandi," I say.

"Jai, weren't you heading out?" She turns to her brother.

"I'm wondering if I should maybe stay home." He folds his arms and gives her a suspicious look.

"Don't be a dick, Jai," she says.

All I can do is stand by as they stare each other down.

"Explain why I shouldn't call Mom and Dad right now and tell them you've got a guy visiting you at home?"

Bollocks, this whole surprise visit thing isn't going as well as I'd hoped.

"Firstly, because that would be really shitty of you, secondly, because maybe one day there will be a time when you need me on your side, and then you'll kick yourself for not being more cooperative right now." She props her arms up on her hips and gives him a dirty look.

"Fine! Jeez. I guess I gotta go then." Mandi's brother shrugs at me, grabs a bundle of keys from the shelf beside the door and heads outside.

Before I get the chance to feel somewhat relieved, Mandi's expression reminds me that I'm still in trouble.

"What the hell were you thinking just turning up here?" she complains under her breath.

"I had to see you." I shrug apologetically. "But it's obvious we can't stay here. Get ready, let's go for a drive. Then you'll be free to tell me all about how I'm a terrible person for visiting you."

She pauses for a moment, then turns back to pick up a handbag from the coat rack on the wall. "Okay. I'm ready."

ONLY A TASTE

We walk back to my car in silence—I sure hope the same nosy neighbor isn't still spying on us now—and get in. That's when I notice how her body language has changed. Although she started off tense; even a bit hostile, now, sitting in the passenger seat of my car, she seems vulnerable. The way she's fidgeting with the hem of her t-shirt suggests she's nervous too. Thank God, it's not just me then.

"Where are we going?" she asks when I turn the key and check my mirrors for non-existent traffic coming up the road from behind.

I hadn't thought of that yet and quickly rack my brain for nice places in the area.

"Iver Heath?" I suggest at last. "We could, uhh... have a picnic?" At least it'll be quiet there. And a reasonable distance from Langley.

She settles back into the plush leather of the seat and rests her hands on her knees as if forcing herself to relax. "I suppose that *would* be nice."

And so that's exactly what we do: head to Iver Heath, only stopping on the way for a few snacks to carry along. It's not much of a drive, and after we've found a suitable place to park, we head into the lush green of the park area, looking for just the right spot.

Any benches near the parking are already occupied. There are families who've had the same idea as us, and the odd couple or single person, taking a rest from walking their dogs.

Finally, beyond the next bend in the walking path, there's an empty spot. Perfect. We sit down and start unpacking the food between us. It's not much, but it's better than nothing. I should've planned for something like this, prepared something special and carried it along, but it's too late for regrets now.

"I'm sorry to just drop in unannounced. I couldn't take it anymore." I look into Mandi's eyes, hoping to see recognition and a reflection of my own desires in there.

She'd been acting weirdly tense throughout our drive, as well as the little walk to get to this bench, but finally, something in her gaze softens. She takes a deep breath, and at last a smile appears on her lips too.

"I know the feeling, it's just... difficult. What if Jai tells on us?" Her eyebrows are pulled together in concern. Being found out is clearly a very big deal to her.

"You were very convincing. About him needing a favor from you in future. I doubt he will rat you out."

"You don't know Jai. We fight a lot."

"He's still your brother." I smile at her. Her frown evens out as she continues to stare back in silence.

Those eyes, those beautiful amber colored eyes, and how the emotions they hold manage to make the hairs on my arm stand up. If we weren't out in a park surrounded by families with small children, I would have been sorely tempted to lift her over my shoulder and have my way with her right here in the bushes behind this bench. But I restrain myself, with difficulty.

"I've really missed you a lot," she whispers at last.

That's what I was waiting for.

"Me too. Talking on the phone doesn't quite do the trick," I say.

She presses her lips together, and scans our surroundings before letting her gaze settle on me again. I love how she looks at me, how she seems to see me for who I am, without showing the slightest interest in all the superficial crap other women I've been with seem to care so much about.

My eyes are drawn to her shapely lips. I so want to taste her lips again.

Mandi subtly leans forward, like she doesn't even realize she's doing it. I can't resist and dive in to steal a kiss. Her arms wrap around my neck and she melts into me. I clear the space between us, causing various little plastic snack containers to end up on the ground.

It doesn't matter. None of it matters. The picnic was just an excuse to be here. I'm not even hungry, not for food, anyway.

I cradle her in my arms, noting how soft and feminine she feels in my embrace. Much more so than in Brighton even. She's curvier than any of my previous flings. I never knew what I was missing.

"Every night I close my eyes and I can't get you out of my head. In the mornings, just before I wake up, I'm back in Brighton, next to you," I mumble.

The words coming out of my mouth seem all jumbled up and senseless now that I've said them out loud, but her gentle moan against my lips suggests they made perfect sense to her.

"I know," she whispers, in between kisses. "Me too."

Our tongues devour each other with an intensity I've never sensed before.

My whole body seems to ache for her attention. I want her to touch me, to soothe me, even if I know that even the slightest caress will set me on fire. Never once have I wanted something—someone—so badly. What a cruel joke that she's been so far away and out of reach ever since that first time.

I wondered earlier today if the weeks we've been apart made me rely on false memories. If seeing her again would disappoint in any way, because the fantasy is better than the reality ever was. There's nothing disappointing about the elegant creature melting against my lips, though. Nothing.

For most of my life—at least ever since I've been able to afford it—I've been all about instant gratification. I've never repressed a single impulse of mine: good food, fine wine, fast cars, and beautiful women. Whatever I desired, I always pursued it until I had it. With her, I find myself ridiculously out of control.

I can't just take her home with me, rip her clothes off and keep her around for my pleasure. Part of me wants just that. Another part of me, one that makes even less sense, threatens to overwhelm me with guilt. I've brought her here today, against her better judgment. If someone she knows spots us and tells her family, she'll be in a whole lot of trouble. And yet, I couldn't stay away any longer. Because I'm selfish.

"Not here," I say, as she slips her hand under my shirt. *Oh God, don't stop.*

"You're right." She sounds breathless as she pulls away, then presses herself against me again for one last kiss. I shouldn't have suggested a picnic at all. Why the hell didn't I take her to a hotel, or somewhere—anywhere—more private? What an idiot I am.

Next time.

"Next time, I'll make sure we're alone," I say.

Her eyes understand, even if our bodies still refuse to step in line and realize that restraint is required. Finally, shrill laughter interrupts us, forcing us to behave ourselves just before the child it belongs to stumbles into view. Shortly after, the little girl's parents follow her on the footpath leading right past our bench.

We awkwardly start picking up the still closed food containers, placing them between us to maintain a safe enough distance. It's time for our so-called picnic.

The food we'd bought in a hurry is tasteless, but the company and innuendo-filled conversation more than make up for it.

CHAPTER THIRTEEN

"Mandeep, open the door!" Dad shouts, his fist banging against the wood.

I jerk up in bed, my heart racing. *Where am I? What's going on?*

"Right now, young lady! Your mother and I want to see you downstairs."

I try to blink the last remnants of drowsiness away and get out of bed. Wonder what's got them all excited so early on a Sunday morning?

Shit, did someone see Callum and me yesterday? That's got to be it. Some nosy neighbor must have seen him around and told on us. Shit, I hate this gossipy neighborhood.

After putting on a robe and heading into the bathroom to splash water on my face, I reluctantly head downstairs. Jai is waiting for me in the hall, shaking his head. Yet, he's not laughing at me for a change. Oh balls, if he can't muster his usual Schadenfreude, things must be serious.

I push open the door, to find Mom, Dad, and Dadi sitting around our impossibly big and chunky dining table. In the center, a glossy magazine.

"Explain yourself!" Dad snaps, tapping his

forefinger impatiently on top of its cover.

That's not mine. And plus, since when are tabloids banned from the house?

I squint and lean ahead to take a better look at it when I see the problem: the cover photo. I choke on my own breath.

The background is familiar, the park where we had our picnic. In the center of the photograph, on the bench, there's Callum with his arm around me. Unlike most tabloid photographs, this one isn't grainy, out of focus, or in any way ambiguous. It's definitely me, smiling up at him. And then there's the headline: *Player both in and out of the kitchen? Notorious bachelor, TV Chef Callum Byrne sighted with mystery squeeze* . Fuck. Fuck! Thank fuck they didn't get a shot of when we made out shortly before this particular shot was taken, but still. FUCK!

"I..."

"You're so screwed," Jai whispers behind me. Thanks. I'd noticed.

"You stay out of it, Jai," Mom scolds him, then turns to face me "What were you thinking, Mandeep? Mrs. Singh just brought this over. Everyone in town talking about it!"

I'm speechless. Of all the ways for them to find out about Callum, with the exception of a leaked sex tape from our night in Brighton, this right here has got to be the worst. I had considered that people from our neighborhood might have seen us. Jai could have ratted us out when Callum first turned up. Maybe I would have been able to explain both of those accusations away, or flat out refuse them.

Not once did I consider the possibility of someone taking our picture and publishing it in a bloody magazine. Can't argue with photographic evidence like this.

"And at a time when we're trying to find you a match? Honestly, I had no idea you hated us this much!" Mom complains.

"Hang on, wait a minute!" I blurt out as my temper gets the better of me. "I never asked for a match! Nobody even thought to ask if I want to get married!"

"Did you hear that, Harry?" Mom turns to face Dad, who looks so furious, little droplets of sweat have collected on his brow. "She doesn't want to get married even! I told you that school was a mistake. We should have sent her to an all-girls school instead, where they teach the kids proper values!"

I roll my eyes and half-turn.

"Not so fast, young lady!" Dad's voice echoes through the room. "Sit down, right bloody now!" He points at the empty chair across from him.

I hesitate, but finally decide to give in. The cat's out of the bag, we might as well have the whole argument right now in one go. Get it over with. Not that I suspect this is something that we will easily resolve.

"How long have you been lying to us? Well?" Dad balls his fist and slams it onto the table, making Mom and me flinch.

"I didn't... I mean..." I stammer.

"How long?" he insists.

"We only just met recently."

"Good, so you can break things off and pray that word hasn't spread too much. Perhaps the Sandhus are still willing to consider the match. Let's hope they don't have a subscription to *Heat* magazine." Mom sits back and folds her arms.

Shuddering at the memory of Diljeet Sandhu, the pathetic guy who couldn't even get a sensible word out with me, I can't hold my tongue. "I'm not marrying that loser!"

"You may not have much of a choice! Your actions will have seriously limited our options! How are we supposed to convince anyone of your suitability as a bride when your face is in all the gossip magazines? They might as well have written right there 'Mandeep Grewal is easy, don't consider her as a bride for your son'!" Mom rants.

Though still in shock, I muster the courage to look around at everyone. Dad looks constipated with rage which is just begging for further release. Mom's part hysterical, part disillusioned.

ONLY A TASTE

Dadi is just sitting quietly with her hands folded together. She's present, but not really involved at this moment. No matter how hard I stare in her direction, she won't look me in the eye. Great, now I've lost my only ally in this house.

"What I don't understand is, what did we do to you to deserve this? You've never wanted for anything: toys, clothes, education. And you repay us like this?!"

"I'm not doing this *to you*!" I sigh and hide my face in my hands. God, this is a disaster.

"Oh yeah?" Mom says, crossing her arms. The angry tears that had collected in her eyes are starting to flow over. Let the guilt trip begin. "We're working our hands to the bone every day to give you and your brother everything we never had, and you turn around and spit in our faces. All the effort we've gone through to find someone nice for you to settle down with. But none of it is good enough. I blame this place. Kids here are so self-entitled!"

"I didn't ask to *settle down* and marry some random stranger I don't even like!"

"If you wanted to find someone for yourself you could have said so. We might have considered that option. But couldn't it at least have been a nice, Punjabi boy?! Someone from our own community?" Mom rants.

As if. When I tried my best to dissuade them from

parading more husband candidates in front of me, they brushed away my concerns like they didn't matter.

"We'll give it a couple of days for things to blow over," Dad says. He still looks furious, and his voice still has that edge to it as well, but he's trying his best to stay calm now. "Then I'll speak to Mr. Sandhu. You can apologize and assure them it was all a misunderstanding and you're not actually... dating... that man."

"What?!" I say.

"You heard me! You'll apologize. Perhaps we can still salvage things."

"Is nobody listening to me? I am *not* marrying that..."

"And you're grounded!"

"Dad, I'm twenty-three!" I complain.

"You should have thought of that before acting out!" Mom butts in.

Why won't they understand that this is nothing to do with them! Why does everything have to be about *them!*

"I mean it. You'll go to work, then come straight home. No more frolicking around the countryside with strange men. As long as you live under this roof, there will be rules to follow," Dad says.

"What are you going to do, throw me out?" My last response passes my lips before I get the chance to reconsider it. Mom's eyes betray shock, while Dad's stare might as well be lethal.

"Enough." Dadi's voice cuts through our continued bickering. "Harpreet. Mandeep. Everyone, enough!"

She hasn't raised her voice much, but it's enough for us to take notice and swallow whatever we were about to say next.

"I'm parched. Let's have some tea." She pushes the chair back. The creak of the wood against the tiled floor makes the hair on the back of my neck stand up.

"I'll get it," I say, jumping up while gesturing at her to sit back down. I rush into the kitchen area and put the kettle on, then line up five cups on the counter. With my back towards everyone, I take a moment to collect myself, dabbing at the tears stuck in my eyelashes with a corner of my t-shirt.

Dad tries to say something but is immediately shushed by Dadi. The exact details of the muffled exchange are drowned out by the gradually increasing hisses from the electric kettle.

To think that only fifteen minutes ago I was blissfully asleep, unaware of the storm brewing downstairs. I stifle a yawn and lean against the counter, letting my head hang down. It's all fucked now. My secret is out.

And there isn't anyone I can talk to about it. Sarah might have been sympathetic, but I did keep Callum's identity from her all this time. That's bound to piss her off; I know I'd be furious. Shit. It seems I'm doomed to suffer through this disaster on my own.

As I pour the hot water into the cups, my vision blurs again. Everything is screwed up. I should have known Callum turning up here was too much of a risk to take. I should have sent him away, but somehow I can't muster the energy to blame him either. This whole thing is my fault, not his.

I should have ignored his first message from a couple of weeks ago. Instead I'd given in to temptation, and now we both have to pay the price.

As soon as it's ready, I carry the cups towards the table, where everyone is avoiding eye contact with me as well as each other. The only person who looks halfway normal is Dadi, who even shoots me a sympathetic smile as she accepts her cup.

"Whatever is going on between you and that man, it's over now," Dad says, while ignoring a disapproving glance from Dadi. "And that's the end of this discussion." He takes a sip of tea and resolutely puts his mug back down, spilling a few drops over the edge.

I guess he's right. Unless I'm willing to choose Callum over them, this is the end for us. Tears start to roll down my cheeks in full force again.

By the time I've somehow made it through my cup of watered down slightly salty tea, the tempers have calmed sufficiently for me to be excused. I head straight up to find my phone blinking with at least a dozen missed calls from Callum, and one solitary message:

'I'm so sorry. Are you OK? C'

I shakily hit 'call' on his number, and nearly choke on my own breath when he answers just moments later.

The conversation that follows passes in a blur of sadness and despair. In between sobs and apologies of my own, I tell him what happened and that I can't do this anymore. We're done.

CHAPTER FOURTEEN

Ever since the whole thing with Callum came out last week, I've tried my best to keep my head down. I've stuck to my decision not to keep in touch with him, no matter how difficult it's been. And I've tried to mend my relationship with Sarah, but it's been a hard slog. In the end, the hopeless romantic in her won out, and she's stopped dodging my calls long enough to tell me to not to give up on true love too quickly... Whatever that means.

What's true love anyway? How many people get together with the best of intentions, only to get a divorce a few years down the line? And that's without the added complications of a very vocal disapproving family. If I choose Callum over them, who is to say I won't regret it and take out my resentment on him later? Plus, I would have to cut off an integral part of my identity and trust that the phantom pain stops after a while. People recover from broken hearts all the time, right? How many people recover from cutting their family out of their lives?

Friends and lovers can come and go. You only get one family in this life.

ONLY A TASTE

All that has been going through my mind during those dark hours when the ticking clock on my bedroom wall is my only companion.

All that, and I don't know if he's actually that serious about me. I don't want to know, because it'll hurt either way.

Every day has been the same. I've tried to just get out of bed in the mornings, go to work, come home, eat, work on a never-ending crochet project I've started just to keep my hands busy, go to bed again. Rinse and repeat, without thinking too much. Only late at night, or at times when I have nothing else to distract me, do I start to wonder *what if.*

It's taken a toll too, the lack of sleep has started to get to me, causing me to just switch off every so often, usually at work. All the numbers on the bills I'm supposed to enter into the accounting system seem to blur and swim on the page. I've taken up drinking multiple cups of coffee every day, instead of tea.

And so about a week passes. I can hardly stand talking to Sarah anymore, because every time I do, she tries to convince me of something or other I should be doing to rescue my relationship with Callum.

Neither do I talk much at home, because every conversation leads to the same place: an interrogation on whether or not I've stopped seeing him.

Thankfully at work, there's no one to talk to.

I idly hover over the 'save' button with my mouse. What else am I supposed to do today after this spreadsheet? I can't remember.

"Mandi, dear?" Mr. Gupta comes up behind me, dragging me out of my late morning vegetative state.

"Yes, Mr. Gupta?"

"I've got to go to the bank this morning and Erica has taken a sick day. Would you be able to keep an eye on the shop for me? Take the laptop down with you if you like."

Fine. Might be an interesting change from being confined to the office.

"Anything in particular I should be doing?"

"I won't be long. If any customer does come in, just do your best to bill them. You do know how the register works, yes?"

I nod. Mom and Dad have one just like it. "No problem."

I lean down underneath my desk to unplug the laptop's charger and gather everything, including the stack of invoices I'd been entering, up in my arms, then follow Mr. Gupta down the narrow staircase to the shop.

"I'll be right back," Mr. Gupta says as he heads out the door.

After a quick look around, I decide to make myself comfortable behind the counter. I'm about to sit back and relax when the bell on the shop door goes off. Is he back already? Did he forget something? I lean forward to get a better look and see that it's not Mr. Gupta at all, but my arch nemesis, Leila, with her best friend Yasmin in tow. Great.

I'm about to duck back and out of view when they notice me.

"Mandi, fancy seeing you here," Leila remarks while flicking her long black hair over her shoulder.

"Leila. Yasmin." I can muster barely a nod. God, please make them go away now.

"So, you're quite the topic of conversation lately..." Yasmin remarks, while folding her arms.

"Oh?" I don't have the energy to pretend, meaning my tone must be dripping in sarcasm.

"Yeah. I've never watched the Good Food channel personally, but somehow it seems a lot more interesting now," Leila says.

I don't respond, meanwhile Yasmin leans over and prods Leila in the side, mumbles something about Callum and 'fat girls', then giggles profusely.

"What was that?" I snap. My patience is running dangerously thin these days. Thanks, sleep deprivation.

They give me a blank stare. Guess they're too chicken to body shame me directly.

"Look, are you actually going to buy something, or are you just here to laugh at me? Because if it's the latter, get it over with quickly, so I can get back to work. Thank you." I fold my arms and glare in their direction.

"Just browsing," Yasmin says, while making a show of herself sifting through one of the racks of sheer baby dolls with lace trim.

"U-huh." I look down at my laptop, and pretend to type something. These people are like vultures, circling around, looking for signs of weakness. When they see you're at your lowest ever, that's when they pounce.

"Actually," Leila says, "what I wanted to say was, good for you."

I can't believe my ears, and look up at the both of them again.

"Hope it works out for you, though I can imagine your parents will have given you quite a bit of shit when those gossip magazines came out." Leila awkwardly shifts her weight from one stiletto-heeled foot to another, then waves at Yasmin and turns to leave the store.

"Uhh, thanks, I guess?" I call out after them.

Wow, that was unexpected.

***

"Hi, Dadi." I give her a quick hug as I enter the living area, then am about to head out and up to my room when she stops me.

"Sit with me." She pats the empty space next to her on the large, brown leather sofa.

I pause, then decide to just do as she says, plopping down beside her with a loud sigh.

"How was your day?" she asks.

"Fine," I respond out of habit. Under normal circumstances I might have told her about Leila coming to the shop, but today I don't have the energy.

"Mhm." She lifts the remote, then switches the channel from the news over to some early evening soap opera.

"You don't look fine."

"Just tired. Had a lot to do at work," I lie. I *am* tired, but I didn't do much all day.

"Well, why don't you have a shower, and wear something nice..." she suggests.

I turn to give her a questioning look. Wear something nice? What a strange thing to say to someone planning to veg out in front of the TV. "Why? What's going on?"

"I tried to talk to him out of it, but your dad had this idea he could not be dissuaded from..."

My heart sinks. *God, now what?* "And?"

"You have a date." Dadi looks straight ahead at the

TV, prompting me to do the same.

This doesn't make any sense.

"A date. With whom?" Please, let it not be that useless boy they were so keen on. Anyone but him.

"His name is Karan, and he does something with electronics, I'm not quite sure."

"But..." I turn to face her again.

"We've been concerned about you, Mandeep. Ever since... you know... you've just withered away. Finally your father has come to the conclusion that he can't just make you marry someone, just because our families are compatible. You have to really like the boy. And apparently that's how these things work here, isn't it? By dating?" Her eyes meet mine, and indeed all I see is concern. She *is* worried about me.

"Yeah, but—" The whole situation is just so outlandish, I can't find the words to argue. They want me to go on a date with some guy they themselves picked out in order to get me to agree to a match? How does that help?

"So tonight it's this boy, Karan. Tomorrow night another one. I've forgotten his name."

I just shake my head. *Unbelievable.*

"That's not how dating works."

"I told you, I tried, but your father has always been extremely stubborn."

Since I don't have the energy to argue, I decide to just do as I'm told. It's not ideal, but what are the chances of this guy being as hopeless as the last one? Low, right?

"Think of it this way, at least you get to go to the movies for free," Dadi calls after me as I head out the living room.

Ugh . This whole plan is ridiculous. And so typical that Dad decided everything and then left it up to Dadi to tell me at the last minute. I can't even argue with her.

Within half an hour, I make sure I'm showered and dressed in a pretty pale blue chiffon dress and heels. I decide not to go overboard with make-up and hair. I don't have time either, because the doorbell rings shortly after I'm somewhat done. *Already?*

Within minutes, Dadi has presumably made it to the door and calls out for me to come down. I reluctantly do so, until she makes a quick escape and I'm face-to-face with a guy who can only be described as *pretty*. Metro-sexual would work too, but mainly just pretty.

"Hi, I'm Mandi." I offer my hand, but he just dives in for a hug and a kiss on each cheek.

"Karan. Nice to meet you."

He smiles widely at me. His cheerfulness is almost contagious.

"Ready to go?" he asks.

I nod and pick up my bag to leave when he pauses in our doorway.

"One thing, just so we're clear." He looks at me a lot more seriously than before.

"Yes?"

"This whole date thing was my mom's idea. Like, she gave me some money even, so I'm like 'OK, great, so we'll go see a movie, have a nice dinner, etc.', but I'm not interested in finding a *girl* to marry." His tone, as well as his exaggerated gesturing makes me smile again. He doesn't need to spell it out, his emphasis on the word 'girl' explains everything.

"I think we're going to get along brilliantly." I instinctively slip my arm into his, just because it seems like the right thing to do somehow, and we're off.

Just like that, and completely unintentionally, Dad's idea has completely paid off for me. For a few hours, I actually feel normal again. By the end of the RomCom we'd decided to see, and after oodles of dinner conversation comparing 'arranged marriage' disaster stories, we agree to tell our folks that our date went horribly.

If nothing else, I may have got a friend out of it though.

CHAPTER FIFTEEN: CALLUM

"Callum, focus!" Trisha pleads with me.

I look up from the notes she's given me, but nothing is sticking.

"Would it help if we took a break?" she asks, her expression somewhere between dejection and sympathy.

"Yeah, let's." I drop the sheet of paper onto the coffee table and get up, heading straight for the kitchen. Chocolate. There should be some chocolate in here somewhere, preferably to be ingested in combination with some caffeine. I press a few buttons and wait as the espresso maker whirs into action, then find an unopened bar of *Lindt* in one of the nearby cupboards.

Today is a new low. Not only am I unable to remember the smallest details Trisha is trying to drill into my head for the upcoming interviews, every time I do try to concentrate, all I can think about is Mandi.

I should have known. I should have expected some bastard paparazzo to come across us sooner or later.

Of course now they're going to ask me about my love life in every upcoming interview too. Trisha has suggested a few phrases for me to fall back on when I feel like telling the interviewer to fuck off and mind their own business. But, I just know my patience will run out and I'll snap sooner or later and resort to more direct language. I feel like cancelling everything, but I'm contractually obligated to follow through with whatever Trisha and the network suggest.

As perfect as everything was when we were together—Mandi and I—our worlds have fallen apart. With her, I could see myself leaving my bachelor days behind me. Now, that hope is gone.

I know she must be hurting a lot too, and that makes it all worse. I know she has feelings for me too, but she's made her choice. I ought to respect that, right? No matter how much it hurts.

"Callum," Trisha calls out for me.

I realize I've just spent the best part of ten minutes staring at my espresso machine, even after it had long finished making my drink.

"Yeah," I respond.

"How about we call it a day, huh? You're clearly distracted. We could just pick this up again tomorrow."

"Fine." I don't even turn around to say goodbye, just continue to stare at the foam-topped black liquid in my cup.

ONLY A TASTE

Mandi made her choice, and I should respect it.

But then again, her decision to call it quits wasn't made voluntarily. *What if...*

I break off a square of dark chocolate and put it in my mouth. It's wonderfully bitter, just like my mood.

What if somehow things could change in our favor... What if her parents could be convinced to give us a chance? What if all it takes is the right approach, the right *gesture?*

Mandi isn't religious, though her family might be. I can relate to the moral restrictions religious people impose on their relationships, I grew up around enough strict Catholics to be able to understand the thought process. We're all sinners in their eyes, so a *real* commitment is required to validate a couple's love in the eyes of God.

Assuming they want what any other parents want—what's best for their child—what could be the reason for them to reject our relationship? Tradition? Culture? *Incompatibility?*

That's got to be it: they want her to settle down with someone with a similar background, because they assume it would make them compatible. But Mandi and I *are* compatible, though. Aren't we? How could I convince them of that?

I think back to my various trips to India. To the people I'd met during my travels, the smells and sights and most importantly, the tastes I'd encountered.

Food tends to be synonymous to culture. This will apply doubly so in the case of Mandi's parents, since they're in the restaurant business as well, and ambitious enough to enter their recipes into various local competitions. *What if I can use that...*

Putting the chocolate back down, as well as the now empty espresso cup, I pick up a notepad and pen and head back to the coffee table to turn on the laptop. Before everything unraveled, I'd made a promise to myself as well as her: that morning in Brighton wasn't goodbye. I was going to pursue her, because I couldn't let go of how she made me feel. To give up now would mean to throw away my last chance to turn things around.

The road ahead might be difficult as well as uncomfortable, but I don't have any other choice. I need her in my life, and I'm willing to fight for the privilege.

****

It takes a couple of days to put my plan into action, but finally, I find myself driving down the same quiet residential road in Langley again. It's a Wednesday, late afternoon, and the clear summer skies of the last time I was here have made way for the cloud cover this damp country is better known for.

There are plenty of empty parking spaces

everywhere, but I decide to take a gamble and park up right outside her front garden. Number seven.

To pretend I'm not nervous at all would be a lie, I'm terrified of what's going to happen. The food aspect I'm not so worried about, I'm confident it's spot on. But there's no way of predicting how everyone will react. The trunk of my car contains a number of gift options, depending on how things go. The most important, as well as the smallest, is safely tucked into my shirt pocket.

Before it's time for any of that, I will need some inside information though. If my assumptions are correct, at this time of day, Mandi's parents should be at the takeaway and she should be at work, leaving only two players at home. Mandi's brother and grandmother. I'll have to win over both of them eventually, or my plan fails.

I walk up the short path and ring the bell, tapping my finger against my thigh restlessly while I wait. It's a fifty-fifty chance as I see it, whether her brother or her grandmother opens up. I'm hoping for the former, to give me an easier way in.

The longer I wait, the less I like my chances.

Finally, as I'm about to turn and head back to the car, the net curtain next to the door stirs. A pair of suspicious eyes, a good foot lower than my eye height peers out. Crap. It's unlikely Mandi's grandmother will be swayed by the bribes I intended to tempt the brother with. I'll be forced to rely on charm instead.

I smile at her nervously, hoping against all hope that she'll actually open the door. The door lock clicks once and indeed, there she is. The old lady looks physically frail, but her eyes command respect. Her stance as well as expression stand in stark contrast with the soft, floral patterned fabric of her traditional clothes, and the wispy white hair that frames her face.

"Mrs. Grewal?" I ask, unnecessarily.

Remembering all my research had taught me, I bend down to touch her feet when she stops me with a pat on the back halfway through.

"Please get up," Mandi's grandmother says.

"My name is Callum B-" I start.

She raises her hand, cutting me short. "I know who you are."

"Although I understand I'm probably not welcome here, I was wondering if I might come in and speak with you."

Her stare could cut through steel, just like Mandi's can, and I instinctively avoid eye contact. The similarities between the two, despite the age difference, are striking.

She leans forward on her walking stick, as if to get a better look at me, then seems to relax just slightly.

"I probably shouldn't say this, but I really enjoy your show," she says.

Looking at her directly again, I see the same subtle

cues that Mandi displays when she's amenable but trying not to let it show. *Whew, she doesn't hate me.* Perhaps all is not yet lost.

"Please come in, have some tea." She gestures at me with her free hand and steps aside to let me enter.

Although I try not to act too intrusive, I can't help myself from having a good look around. The decor is a throwback to the seventies, except for the open plan kitchen which looks like it has been renovated within the past few years. The heavy wooden furniture, along with the patterned rug in the living area and busy wallpaper all round remind me of when I moved in with my grandma after Mom and Dad had their accident. She favored a similar style.

"Can I help at all?" I ask, when I hear the electric kettle start up in the kitchen.

"Please take a seat." She gestures at the dining table, rather than the sofa in the living area, so I pull out a chair and wait. My hands are damp with nervous sweat, so I make a few half-hearted attempts to dry them on my trousers. She's let me into the house, so far so good, and she likes my TV persona at least. But there's still a lot of scope for things to go horribly wrong from here.

Looking around the room, I notice the many framed pictures of the various members of the Grewal family. Mandi and her brother, from a few years ago. Another frame displays a couple—

presumably Mandi's parents—at work in a small commercial kitchen. Yet another shows the same couple, a few decades younger: her in a traditional red bridal outfit, and him in an ornate suit type thing with a color coordinated turban. The one thing that strikes me is how little her dad has changed between the two photographs. It must be the beard and turban, which make him look fierce as well as ageless.

When Mandi's grandmother returns, I get up briefly to accept my tea. She sits opposite me with a cup of her own, wrapping her hands carefully around the hot porcelain.

"What is it you wanted to say—may I call you Callum?"

"Of course, yes. Well, I know that you don't approve of my relationship with Mandi."

"Our traditions differ quite a bit from the norm in this country when it comes to relationships."

"Indeed, and I completely understand. Which is why I wanted to explain my intentions."

"I'm listening." She folds her hands and keeps her eyes completely focused on me.

"Despite what the papers may say about me, I'm very serious about your granddaughter. I care for her a great deal, and it is really unfortunate things had to come out the way they did." I take a sip of tea, while finding the right words for what I really want to say.

"What I really would like is a chance to prove

myself to you, and Mandi's parents also. If you still disapprove, that's fine—I mean not fine, I'd be devastated—but at least I know that I will have done everything in my power to turn this situation around." I'm rambling. This isn't good.

Mrs. Grewal's expression is hard to read as she continues to keep me in her sights.

"What exactly did you have in mind?" she asks at last. The slight sparkle in her eye suggests I may just have at least one member of the Grewal family already on my side before I've even put the rest of my plan into action.

As I explain my ideas, she mostly nods in agreement, jumping in with the occasional suggestion.

There may just be a chance this works out.

Mandi will be home at five, and Mandi's grandmother will call her parents back from the takeaway around that time too. It would be ideal if they arrive at the same time, just so it doesn't feel like a complete ambush.

We'll have tea and snacks ready, and hope for the best.

CHAPTER SIXTEEN

When I walk home from work, the skies overhead signal a change. The unusually warm weather is about to make way for what an English summer is more known for: endless grey skies and regular showers. I speed up, in the hopes that I can beat the first drops.

The wind picks up as I turn into our street, encouraging me to walk even faster. But then, something stops me in my tracks. The spot outside our house where Dad normally parks is occupied by another car, a sports car. My heart skips a few beats.

What the fuck is Callum doing here? Did he not get the message? Does he not realize how much trouble I'm going to be in?

Walking past the silver grey coupe, I note that it's empty. Fuck. He didn't go inside, did he? At least Mom and Dad aren't home this time of day, but Dadi is!

I reluctantly approach the front door, key in hand, listening out for voices. Once I enter, I hear a muffled conversation coming from the living area. Shit. My heartbeat is going into overdrive and panic threatens to wash over me. Why didn't he just listen to me? Why come here?

ONLY A TASTE

When I open the door, I'm faced with a sight I never expected to see: Dadi and Callum sitting at our dinner table, having a seemingly pleasant chat over tea and sweets.

"Mandi!" Callum gets up to greet me, but I avoid eye contact with him.

"What's going on? Why are you here?" I wrap my arms around myself, as if to protect me from the inevitable fallout of his actions.

"Sit down, Mandeep." Dadi gestures at the chair next to Callum, then slides over an empty cup. There's a teapot in the center of the table. She nods at me to serve myself.

We never use that teapot except when we have guests Mom wants to impress...

"They'll be here any minute now," Dadi remarks while glancing at the wall clock behind me.

Oh God, please let this not mean what I think it means?

Sure enough, within moments, the front door clicks open and footsteps as well as voices enter the hallway, heading right for us.

The door swings open and in comes Dad, who can't hide his shock at seeing Callum sitting between me and Dadi at our table.

"What is the meaning of all this?" he booms.

"What? Oh my!" Mom exclaims as she enters the room just behind him.

"Harpreet, please take a seat, have some tea. Listen to what the boy has to say," Dadi speaks calmly.

"How dare you invite him here, after embarrassing us by having your picture taken together?" Dad rants at me.

I press my lips together tightly, unsure of what to say.

"She didn't know, she's only just come home from work as well," Dadi explains. "Sit down. Listen to him."

I steal a glance at Callum, who looks wooden and tense as he gets up off his chair.

"Mr. Grewal," he starts, stretching his right hand out in an attempted handshake.

Dad glares back and forth between Callum, me and Dadi, his eyes bulging. "You're not welcome in my house."

"Harpreet!" Dadi raises her voice, making all of us flinch. "This is my house too. Sit down!"

Mom takes the lead, walking around the table to take a seat opposite me. I dare not look directly at her. Not knowing what else to do, I pick up two empty cups that were already laid out on the table and pour the tea.

After staring all of us down, Dad finally follows, taking a seat beside Dadi. Callum sits down last.

"Mr. Grewal, I understand that we all started off on the wrong foot. And I do apologize for visiting your home unannounced."

Dad shoots me an angry look and shakes his head. I'm so done.

"Mandi- Mandeep did not know about any of this. We haven't spoken in a week."

Callum slides the tray of traditional Indian sweets over towards Mom and Dad. The selection of laddoos and burfis looks familiar as well as alien. They don't look like they came from any of the shops around here.

"Thank you," Mom whispers, while picking up a laddoo almost on autopilot. She's never been good at resisting temptation. I get my sweet tooth from her.

"I know you object to our relationship. I think I understand your reasons."

"Then why are you even here?" Dad says, while waving away the tray Callum is now holding in his direction.

"To show you that I have nothing but good intentions. To hopefully address some of your concerns."

"Right." The sarcasm in Dad's voice is obvious to me, I wonder if Callum hears it too.

I don't know what to expect, but I'm not holding out much hope. As Dadi has made it clear on numerous occasions, my Dad is the most stubborn person she knows. Some idle talk over tea and treats is not going to sway him. No way.

"I have great respect for your culture, your traditions."

"And what do you know of our culture?" Dad snaps, and is instantly met with a stern look from Dadi.

"I've travelled extensively in India, I've always been fascinated by the food anyway. The diversity. Then again, it's necessary to understand the people, the traditions, in order to make sense of the food."

"And?" Dad, who seems to have calmed down just slightly, sits back in his chair and finally takes a first sip from his cup.

"You're concerned about the happiness and well being of your daughter, that much is obvious. You want her to be with someone who will take care of her, understand her, provide for her and any future children, correct?"

"That's right."

"You are looking for someone who is compatible with her as well as your family. Someone who believes in keeping promises and commitments, who won't just run away when things get tough as they inevitably must in life."

"Yes."

"I love your daughter more than anything in the world." Callum's words seem to echo around the room.

I can't believe he just said that! And to my Dad, no

less.

Shocked, I turn to stare at Callum. I've got to be hallucinating. This stuff doesn't happen in real life, just in movies.

"I can provide for her, take care of her. I think I understand her at least a little and I believe us to be compatible. The rest, I'm willing to learn. You see, I didn't tell her I was coming here today, because I knew she would have dissuaded me. We shouldn't have been hiding our relationship from you. That was wrong and disrespectful. I deeply apologize for that."

Dad scoffs, but then takes another sip of tea, seemingly relaxing just a little bit more. It's the calm before another storm, isn't it? It has to be just a matter of time before he loses his patience and kicks Callum out of the house once and for all.

"You see, where I grew up in Ireland, family is all-important. Family, and the church. I believe we share a lot of the same values, even if our religions and origins differ. My parents passed when I was quite young, and ever since then I really missed the feeling of being part of a close-knit family. I've had more professional success than I could ever dream of, but I never had that same feeling of belonging which you can only get from your family. Until I met Mandeep."

Although I knew about his parents, he'd told me about growing up with his grandmother, I never quite understood properly how that would have affected him. Having to speak about it so openly must be very difficult, especially when faced with someone like my dad. I reach over under the table, placing my hand on his thigh.

"I realized that that's why I was drawn to her in the first place. Because the warm loving relationship you all share has shaped her into the sort of person she is today."

I can't believe what I'm hearing.

"The tabloids may be full of nonsense about me, but deep down, we're not so different. From the moment Mandeep and I met, I knew that my search was over. That I'd never look at another woman. Never betray or abandon her. I knew that she's everything I'd been looking for my whole life."

Callum takes a deep breath, and straightens his back before continuing. "Mr. Grewal, with your blessing, I would like to start a family of our own with her." Callum glances at me for a short moment, I shoot him a subtle smile. Despite all the messages back and forth, and the way he reacted to me when we went on that ill-fated picnic, I had no idea he felt this deeply about me.

"I'm here to ask for your permission to marry your daughter. Which, in the Catholic tradition is considered to be life-long promise before God."

Callum's hand finds mine, cupping it protectively, but his gaze is firmly fixed on Dad's face. In fact everyone, including myself, is now staring at Dad. My heart is hammering in my throat. That was pretty convincing, wasn't it? But there's no accounting for Dad's stubbornness.

Mom places her hand on Dad's, which is resting beside his cup of tea. Meanwhile Dad is glaring back at Callum.

Minute after minute passes in silence.

Finally, it's Dadi who can't take it any longer. "I think he makes a good case. It takes courage to come here and make a stand like this," she says.

Dad stirs, but only to pick up his cup, emptying it with one last swig. "I think." He clears his throat. The suspense is killing me.

"At this point, it's clear that it no longer matters what *I* think," he grumbles.

I'm shocked. All that, and he's not even going to answer Callum?

"What do you think? Are *you* convinced?" Dad asks me.

I don't know what to say, I just stare at him with my mouth agape. The room starts to spin around me, and I'm not sure where to look or what to say.

Then Callum gets up next to me, diverting my attention away from Dad. With my hand still in his, Callum gets down on one knee on the ground and retrieves something from his shirt pocket. Holding it up closer to me, I can see that it's a little velvet box.

"Mandi, I know this is sudden, and probably not how you expected this would go, but I meant everything I just said. I love you, and I always will. Will you marry me? Whenever you're ready, of course."

I cover my mouth with my free hand, and stare down at the little box, which Callum opens up to reveal a very sparkly diamond ring. It's beautiful, with its intricate floral design in gold, and diamonds small and large mounted in the center. The whole scene gives me goose bumps.

From the corner of my eye, I notice Mom dabbing at the corners of her eye with her scarf. She's always been the emotional one. Dad is still being his stern self, but at least his eyes are no longer shooting daggers.

"Well, answer him!" Dadi urges.

Tears well up and my throat threatens to close, but I force myself to answer anyway.

"Yes," I whisper. "Yes!"

Callum lets go of my hand, then takes the ring out of its little holder. His hands tremble as he slides it onto my ring finger. Dadi claps her hands. I don't remember seeing her this happy in quite a while. Mom now has tears streaming down her face openly and has given up on trying to dry them. Even Dad, who rarely shows any emotion at all, seems affected. His eyes have softened, and in a strange twist of fate,

I think I can even spy a little smile peeping through his thick beard.

I look down at the ring on my finger, and it strikes me that although I've spent the best part of this month fighting tooth and nail to avoid getting married, actually, it's not the idea of marriage that I took issue with. Just as long as I'm marrying the right man.

"Well then. Everyone have something sweet!" Dadi says. Can't argue with that.

"These laddoos are really lovely. Where did they come from anyway?" Mom asks, picking up another one of the spherical sweets.

I follow her example, wondering the same thing.

Callum, who takes a seat next to me again, says, "I took the liberty of trying out a recipe that was given to me during my last visit to India."

"Wow, you made these?" I ask.

"You do realize he's a chef, right?" Dadi teases me.

"Yeah, but..."

Before I get the chance to finish my thought, the door swings open dramatically.

"Hey, did you see the sweet-ass ride parked outside our house?" Jai asks, while wandering into the room, until he finally notices Callum and stops dead in his tracks. "Oh, shit."

"Language!"Dadi scolds him.

"Sit down," Dad says. "Have some tea."

"Okay..." Jai eyes Callum and me curiously while making his way to the other end of the table, towards the only empty chair. "What's going on?"

"We've agreed on a match for Mandeep," Mom says in the most matter-of-fact tone she can muster.

"Well I'll be da-" Jai swallows the end of his sentence and scrutinizes me with one eyebrow cocked. "I mean, congratulations, I guess?"

"Cheers," I remark dryly.

Although he's still in shock, I can see it in his eyes that Jai understands how huge this is. A massive step, that'll have implications for him, too, a few years down the line. Whenever it'll be his turn to settle down.

EPILOGUE

The wedding preparations had taken up the best part of two months.

We were in a hurry, Callum and I. Although my folks had finally agreed to see things my way, they weren't about to let their daughter go off and spend a lot of alone time with a man, even if he was her fiancé. *What would people say?*

But the wait is finally over. The actual wedding took place earlier today at the Sikh temple Mom and Dad regularly attend. Now the reception—to which Mom insisted on inviting the entire neighborhood—Callum and I have officially been announced as husband and wife.

Nobody can come between us anymore.

Looking across the room at Callum, I'm relieved that he seems in his element. Especially considering the entire thing—including catering—was totally planned out by my parents, according to our customs and traditions. He's been a very good sport about it all; he even grew a bit of a beard and agreed to wear a turban just for the ceremony earlier.

He really meant it when he said that family was important to him. So, considering he doesn't have one of his own, he's been solely focused on keeping mine happy.

Most of the guests have already gone, leaving only a select few relatives and close friends. One of whom, Sarah, comes up to me holding a gift bag.

"I wanted to give this to you now, rather than you know, in front of everyone." She winks at me when she hands me the present.

I smile at her. "Thanks."

Even though I'd told her she should wear whatever she was comfortable with, she insisted on buying herself a pale pink and silver saree just for tonight. It's strange, seeing her dressed like this, but she's managed to carry it off extremely well.

"Well, take a peek," she encourages me.

I push aside the tissue paper covering the top of the bag and reach inside until my fingertips touch what feels like soft, silky lace. A quick look reveals it's indeed lingerie. Very romantic, very bridal.

"Neither of us could get away with wearing white at our wedding, strictly speaking. But that doesn't mean we shouldn't make an effort." Sarah grins at me.

Good thinking. In all the rush to make it through the day, I hadn't planned or prepared anything for when it's all over and Callum and I are finally alone together.

"Thank you so much. I think we'll get some good use out of this," I remark.

"I know you will. Slut."

"Whore."

After all the weirdness our friendship went through lately, finally the air seems clear between us again. She might be a newly employed tabloid journalist now, but she vowed to keep today's festivities entirely off the record. And I trust that she will.

We share a final giggle, then she hugs me goodbye. Sarah turns around and waves one last time before finally leaving the banquet hall as well.

"What was that all about?" Callum asks, resting his hand on my shoulder.

"You'll soon find out." I smile at him naughtily. *And I can't wait to see your face when you do.*

"Well then, let's not delay things too much," Callum says, as his gaze lingers on my lips.

I survey the room, spotting Mom and Dad speaking to Mr. and Mrs. Gupta, who appear to be leaving as well. Dadi is sitting at a table just off the side of the two of them, looking content, if tired.

"Let's excuse ourselves." I take Callum's hand and we walk over towards them to say our goodbyes. They exchange a look of understanding, then Mom hugs the two of us, one after the other, and Dad shakes Callum's hand, before protectively resting his hand on the top of my head. It took a little time, but Callum's absolute persistence and tireless efforts to find common ground between himself and my folks has borne fruit. They've finally accepted him as part of the family. Something I never thought could really happen.

We agree to meet in the morning at the breakfast buffet, before it's time to check out and make our way back home. Only, of course, my home won't be in Langley anymore...

After a quick honeymoon, the destination of which has still been kept from me, I'll move into Callum's place in the city. And then, who knows? I'm definitely not going to be working for Mr. Gupta anymore, or do anything else that has been pre-decided for me by my parents. From here on out, I finally get to be an adult. With Callum by my side, I finally get to make my own choices. I can't wait.

As we walk out of the hall, and down the corridor leading to the stairs, I keep stealing glances at him. I can't believe this has actually happened. And without any further drama, too. Even Leila was on her best behavior when she came by with her parents earlier.

We make it to our room, and Callum uses his keycard to unlock the door. He releases my hand and in one swift move, scoops me up into his arms to carry me over the threshold. Shocked as well as impressed by his strength, I can't stop giggling. I wrap my arms around him, gift bag still in hand behind his back, and rest my head against his shoulder. He's quite something; my *husband.*

It's weird, thinking of Callum in those terms... I guess I have a few things to get used to as well going forward.

"You want to tell me what's in the bag now?" He asks me as he carries me through the spacious room and towards the huge four poster bed, which has been decorated with flowers and rose petals by the hotel staff.

I shake my head.

"You want to tell me where we're going tomorrow?" I counter.

He lays me down on the covers, and takes a step back to admire the view. "You're going to have to wait and see. I want to surprise you."

"Mhm." I grin at him.

Before tiredness gets the chance to overwhelm me, I get up and head into the en-suite, still clutching Sarah's gift bag in my hand. I kick off my heels and do my best to quickly get out of the heavily embroidered red silk saree—the same my mom had worn on her big day—before folding it and carefully draping it over the bathtub.

Next I strip down the rest of the way, removing jewelry as well, and put on the white lace corset and panty set Sarah gifted me. A quick glance in the mirror confirms that everything about it is just perfect. She knows her lingerie, Sarah does. You can tell that she used to work at *Victoria's Secret* when we first met in college.

When I slowly push my way through the door and back into our room, I see Callum sitting on the edge of the bed already, waiting for me. I pose in the doorway, drawing the moment out as long as I can. He's significantly less patient than me, and manages to get up while removing his coat, as well as his trousers before he even reaches me.

What a fine specimen of a man he is. Of course I knew that much already, from the moment I first saw him on the promenade in Brighton. But in an effort to respect my parent's wishes, we haven't seen each other alone like this in months, and the anticipation is killing me. Now, though, he's *all mine*.

"You look beautiful," he whispers, while nuzzling my neck.

"You're not so bad yourself," I respond, doing my best not to whimper when he starts to kiss me in that spot where I'm most sensitive, just below my earlobe.

"Will you join me on the bed, dear wife?" he asks, taking a step back while holding onto my hand.

I can't suppress a laugh, despite or perhaps because he looks so serious calling me that. It sounds bizarre to my ears. Callum and I; husband and wife.

"Of course, beloved husband."

He grins back at me, and takes another step closer to the bed behind him. I follow.

ONLY A TASTE

When he sits down on the edge, I straddle him, wrapping my arms around his neck again like when he carried me over the threshold. We share a kiss, which doesn't relieve the tension building between us for the past two months, as much as heightens it even further.

I need him. He needs me.

His hands roam my body, reclaiming what had previously already been his. This time, all I feel is unadulterated pleasure, no longer hindered by the little voice of a guilty conscience, that never fully left me the first time we did this.

Not everyone may approve of our choices, as some of the cooler faces around the room at tonight's reception already made abundantly clear. But, it's official now. We will never need to hide our relationship ever again.

I give in to his embrace and we both fall back onto the bed. He cups my face and kisses me more deeply, his tongue devouring mine with the kind of passion I'd never encountered before meeting him. Our first time was already special, but tonight will be all the more so because it's no longer illicit and forbidden.

Everything about this moment feels *right*. And it doesn't need to end, ever. Tomorrow, when we wake up together, neither of us has to leave the other. Neither of us has to worry about being found out. Well, except by the tabloids perhaps.

We'd done our best to keep the venue a secret by keeping his name out of the booking. But, someone always talks, Callum said. They'll probably be here tomorrow, hoping to find out every last detail about our relationship and get some candid photos of the two of us together. We intend to sneak out early to avoid them, but you never know.

I make my way down his body, tasting skin as I go along. I've craved this moment with all my being ever since our first time three months ago. The longest and most difficult wait of my life.

He's fit, with well-toned abs and a beautifully sculpted chest that could inspire jealousy in a Greek god. Unlike me; my figure is a lot softer and more curvaceous. Plenty of people advised me to go on a crash diet; to trim down for my big day. I was right to ignore them. The way Callum looks at me wipes any last shred of doubt from my mind. He loves me unconditionally. Just how I am.

Lust takes over as I make it further down his body. Caressing, and tasting perfectly smooth skin as I go.

I gesture at him to lie down flat and put his legs up on the bed. He does. I sit beside him and enjoy how every touch of mine makes his body tremble ever so slightly. This tense anticipation feels delicious, for him as well as me. I love how he's already hard, and actually shudders when I close my fingers around his length. He doesn't say a word, just groans once when

I lean down and take him between my lips.

Every thought left in my mind serves to give him pleasure.

How to lick his shaft and then close my lips around the tip of his cock becomes second nature. He tastes perfect: clean, with a hint of saltiness; like the fresh sea air in Brighton.

I speed up, taking more of him into my mouth with each stroke, and rejoice how his body tenses every time I suck. I'm just getting into a faster rhythm when only minutes later his hand finds the back of my neck and freezes there.

"Stop," he gasps.

"Mm?" I look up at him, his expression tells me I have him right where I want him now. Struggling for self-control.

"Not yet," he says.

I decide to give in to his request. Just this once.

As soon as I lie down on my back next to him, he takes over. He rolls onto his side, then on top of me, and kisses me yet again. It's a desperate kiss, so urgent it's almost painful, but in a good way. He takes my breath away when his hand infiltrates my most intimate folds, playing, manipulating me, turning the tables on me.

My eyes close involuntarily as I am taken over by pleasure. Soon, we'll be joined fully. I'll be his, and he'll be mine, unconditionally.

He spreads my legs and enters me unsheathed. We both want a family eventually, though we've agreed to wait for the right time. But because we'd wanted our wedding night to au naturel, I'd started taking the pill to prepare. Gone is the need for barriers; rubber or otherwise.

Despite being sopping wet already, his cock stretches me out until it burns a little. The pleasure is so intense, it makes me cry out. Funny, how different it feels without a condom. How different it feels when you're married.

"I'm not hurting you, am I?" he asks.

I just shake my head and smile, but am mute otherwise. It's too intense and sensitive; too beautiful for words.

He pushes into me deeper and deeper with every move. I don't know what else to do but claw at his back every time he withdraws. I want more; so much more of everything he has to offer. He can see it in my eyes and is intent on giving it to me.

The heavy bed creaks under the intensity of our movements, but neither of us pay it any mind.

My consciousness is reaching another plane, one where petty concerns about furniture lose all relevance. As he continues to claim me—the term 'making love' would be woefully inaccurate for what's going on right now—my vision starts to blur. I can't focus on anything else anymore, just the in and out, the relentless rhythm of his hips as they goad me towards my release.

A sweet, tingly feeling spreads through my body, projecting outward from my lower abdomen, and yet staying largely in that part of my body. Until... His gasps fill the room, along with my moans. If another guest hears us, so be it.

He fucks me harder yet again, flicking his hips upwards at the end of each thrust. A thin coat of sweat covers my body, not because I'm hot or even tired, but just because I'm so close I can almost taste it.

As he leans on one arm, the other hand reaches between us again, this time going for my nipple. He tweaks and teases me, starting softly and then growing more daring when I thrash about underneath him. I need his body closer to mine, and I can't control myself anymore, clawing at him again to get him into a tighter embrace.

With one final scream, my body signals it's time. I freeze, but he struggles on despite me keeping him almost in a stranglehold. The next two, three, four thrusts threaten to make me cry. My eyes do moisten at last, such is the intense pleasure I feel.

I don't want him to see, but I'm powerless over my own body.

"I love you," I gasp, but I'm not sure he even hears me.

He grinds to an abrupt halt himself, his body shuddering against me as he reaches his own peak. The formerly rock solid muscles in his arm soften, and he lowers himself onto me.

I keep him there, lying in my arms with his head on my shoulder, for as long as we need to calm our breaths.

"I love you too," he finally responds, minutes later.

He leans up, then wipes the wetness off my face with his thumb. I worried it would ruin this moment if he noticed my tears, but the smile on his lips tells me he understands. From now on, I'll be forever understood.

I smile back at him, but then remember the one thing that's still nagging at me, despite everything.

"Won't you please tell me where we're going in the morning? It's going to come out at the airport anyway..." I beg.

His gaze rests on mine for a moment, then on my lips. He kisses me once more, as if to silence me, but then he leans back up and reconsiders.

"You're assuming our honeymoon will involve an airport," he teases.

"Well... doesn't it?"

"Okay, fine. There really was only one choice."

"Which is?" I ask. *One choice? What is he talking about?*

"When you said back in Brighton after we'd just

met, that you'd never been to India yourself... Well... As I said, no other choice."

Other girls might have hoped for Caribbean palm trees and cocktails on the beach, but somehow, the fact that he remembered that little detail from when we first met means everything. I smile up at him, grateful for the surprise, even if I forced him to reveal it early.

"India. Wow. That's going to be amazing!"

"It's only the beginning."

I nod and let the beautiful blue depths of his eyes capture me. This *is* only the beginning.

The beginning of our adventures together. And, the beginning of our wedding night. After three months of forced celibacy, we still have a lot of catching up to do. The way he's staring at me now with renewed hunger in his gaze tells me we're exactly on the same page.

***

AUTHOR'S NOTE

Thanks so much for reading *Only a Taste!*

This, the third of the Chance Encounters series of stand-alone novellas is different from the other two, not just because it features the first multicultural pairing I've written about so far, but also for how it came into being. Both *One Night Stand* and *Beautiful Stranger* started ages ago as short stories, which I then developed into novellas. *Only a Taste* was conceived as a novella from the beginning. While I was writing *One Night Stand* (If you haven't read it yet, don't worry, I won't mention any spoilers), I came up with two minor characters: Jack Cleary who plays the role of Lucy's nightmare client, and his friend and colleague, Callum Byrne. They're both renowned chefs with their own restaurants. I couldn't wait to incorporate these people into stories of their own, but I wasn't quite sure how to go about it, because obviously in order for romance to occur, every hero needs a heroine...

Enter Mandi. I've been exposed to Indian (specifically Punjabi) culture quite a bit, so it was just a matter of time for me to include that in my writing. Although I'm not Indian myself, I can relate to the feeling of growing up as somewhat of an outsider, a second generation immigrant. My childhood was spent juggling two identities, including different languages: my family's origins, versus the local culture where we lived. It's not always easy to figure out where you belong, when your family and friends seek to pull you in differing directions. I can also relate to the difficulty one may face when marrying outside of one's own ethnicity or religion.

Since all the Chance Encounters books feature real places in South-East England, I started brainstorming areas that I was at least somewhat familiar with. That's how the pieces started to come together. I know Slough and the surrounding areas well enough, and it just so happens that a lot of people of Punjabi origins live around there. I like throwing opposites together, so why not Callum Byrne, the Irish TV Chef who managed to build up a nice little career for himself in the UK, and a second generation British Asian girl from Langley whose difficulties finding a job after University meant she's forced to move back in with her parents. It seemed like a great opportunity to tell a story of clashing cultures.

Obviously that's the main conflict of this story: the clash between Mandi's conservative family and her own identity as an independent and free-spirited British woman. In her mind, her self-worth doesn't depend on how soon (or how well) she marries, she's perfectly content being herself. Her family, though, don't quite agree and would rather see her settled as soon as possible. Because that's what good girls do.

In such situations it would be easy for an outsider to say 'well it's *your life,* so just do what *you* want'. In reality though, having to go against everything your parents believe in, effectively giving them the middle finger, would be extremely difficult and painful. It's a lot easier said than done. Mandi feels stuck initially, she wants nothing more than for everyone to just get along, or at least for her worlds to continue coexisting without much overlap like while she was still living on her own during her studies. I hope I was able to portray her struggle accurately, based on what I've seen other people go through when they tried to go against tradition in their love life.

Meanwhile, Callum, with his money and fame, has never really had to fight for attention. He sees Mandi as a challenge initially, but then realises that their attraction runs a lot deeper. Despite everything, he's a true romantic at heart, he just never found the right person to bring to light that aspect of himself. In Mandi, he finds the girl he wants to settle down with. His money and success don't impress her much, which helps keep their relationship interesting. There's nothing more boring in the long term than to be with someone who agrees with or loves everything you do.

So that's what makes him willing to change for her. To ignore the customs of dating and relationships in the western world which expect that you spend a long time figuring out whether you're right for one another. You might even live together before even considering popping the question. With Mandi, that's not an option, because her parents will never accept him if he approaches their relationship from that angle. So if you feel you're right for one another, why not make a big commitment? He stands to lose the one chance to create a family with the only girl that's ever interested him like that, if he doesn't at least try.

Anyway, so those were my inspirations and I hope you enjoyed the story as much as I did while writing it. If you're interested in reading more of my work, perhaps you'll consider signing up for my newsletter. I'll even give you a free book of your choice when you sign up!

x, Lorelei

- ❖ LMoone.com
- ❖ Lorelei Moone on Facebook
- ❖ AuthorLMoone on Instagram

I also write Paranormal Romance as Lorelei Moone. Check out LoreleiMoone.com for more information.

SPECIAL OFFER!

For a limited time, all new mailing list subscribers will receive a FREE short story, called At First Sight.

Claim your free copy here:

LMoone.com

Look for the newsletter sign-up form on the right hand side of the page.

OTHER PUBLICATIONS

<u>Big Boys Do It Better Series:</u>
Recipe for Passion
Paperback ISBN: 9781913930547
Best Friends Forever
Paperback ISBN: 9781913930554

<u>The Chance Encounters Series:</u>
One Night Stand
Paperback ISBN: 9781913930080
Beautiful Stranger
Paperback ISBN: 9781913930103
Only a Taste
Paperback ISBN: 9781913930127

<u>The Undateables Series:</u>
The Rebound List
Paperback ISBN: 9781913930042
Sally
Paperback ISBN: 9781913930066

<u>As Lorelei Moone:</u>

<u>The Scottish Werebears Series:</u>

An Unexpected Affair

Paperback ISBN: 9781913930165

A Dangerous Business

Paperback ISBN: 9781913930172

A Forbidden Love

Paperback ISBN: 9781913930189

A New Beginning

Paperback ISBN: 9781913930196

A Painful Dilemma

Paperback ISBN: 9781913930202

A Second Chance

Paperback ISBN: 9781913930219

<u>The Alpha Squad Series:</u>

Boot Camp

Paperback ISBN: 9781913930233

Friends & Foes

Paperback ISBN: 9781913930240

Infiltrator

Paperback ISBN: 9781913930257

Showdown

Paperback ISBN: 9781913930264

<u>**The Vampires of London Series:**</u>

Alexander's Blood Bride

Paperback ISBN: 9781913930288

Michael's Soul Mate

Paperback ISBN: 9781913930295

Lucille's Valentine

Paperback ISBN: 9781913930301

<u>**The Shifters of Black Isle Series:**</u>

Claimed by the King

Paperback ISBN: 9781913930325

The Soldier and the Siren

Paperback ISBN: 9781913930332

A Dragon's Treasure

Paperback ISBN: 9781913930349

The Warlock's Conquest

Paperback ISBN: 9781913930356

www.ingramcontent.com/pod-product-compliance
Lightning Source LLC
Chambersburg PA
CBHW071002180726
48291CB00004B/1405